# A WINTER OF ROMANCE

SHERYLYNNE L. ROCHESTER

SHEKINAH PUBLICATION & COMMUNICATIONS, INC.

# CONTENTS

## PRAYERS

# CHAPTER 1

The sound of sweet silence nestled in the background as I sat enjoying winter. I smiled watching the beautiful scenery through my window. Snow covered everything, and all I thought about was how I loved this time of the year.

As the snow continued to fall, I sipped some hot chocolate while writing in my journal and praying to God. It relaxed me and I wish it didn't have an end. I looked at the clock realizing I had to finish up this entry before work. I jotted down the last of a small prayer for my future husband:

*May you always feel the same faith and love I do when I think of our great God. It's a beautiful morning He alone created. I pray many blessings on you this day, my dear husband.*
*Forever and always,*
*Addison*

I pulled back and looked at the prayer and nodded, satisfied with it. As I closed my prayer journal, I looked up to the heavens and closed my eyes. This overwhelming sensation of peace came over me as I prayed another prayer for myself to God.

*Father,*

*Thank you for your great love and for the care you've given me throughout the years. Thank you for always giving me unfailing love. I am so glad to know your love never fails.*

*Today, I pray that you will continue to help me wait for my future husband to come my way. For I know that those who wait on the Lord shall renew their strength; they shall mount up with wings like eagles, they shall run and not be weary, they shall walk and not faint. Lord, please remind me of this when the wait is getting too long for me.*

*Right now I ask that you lead and guide me to the right man You have for me. I also ask that you renew my spirit, fill me with Your peace and help me to always leap for joy as I wait.*

*I love You and I thank you. I ask these things in Jesus' Name, Amen.*

Over the years since I was sixteen, this journal has helped me deal with being single. I find peace in knowing someday, I will share them with the man I love. Now I'm twenty-nine and still looking for that special someone, I know that God is the one that will help him find me. Then, on our wedding day, I'll be able to give him these prayers and journal entries.

I placed the journal in its secure hiding spot. I couldn't wait for the day my future husband read my thoughts and my payer. As I thought about it, I heard my cell phone ringing.

"Hey, Brianna," I said, answering the phone call.

"Hey, Addison, I need a favor," she said with urgency.

She was six years younger than I was and a single mother. Her boyfriend left her the minute he found out she was pregnant. That left her sixteen, pregnant, and alone. With the help of our mother, she took care of him with no problems. Our mom died a year earlier on Christmas Day and after, I saw my sister go on a downward spiral. My sister needed me and I would be there for her always.

"Sure, what is it?" I asked, putting on my chipper attitude, as I waited to see what she needed this time.

"I have a job interview and I can't be late for it, but that means I need someone to take Jack to school. Please, I know I ask a ton of you, but I need your help today. Plus, I would love to send out a few more resumes."

I wanted Brianna to find a job. It was a huge step of making sure she could provide for Jack. Besides, I loved taking care of my nephew, so there was no doubt I would accept the responsibility.

"You're on your way?" I asked.

"I'll be there in ten minutes," she said.

"Okay, I'll take him to school," I said.

She always gave the same story and excuse every time. She was always appreciative, but she never wanted to change. Yet, I couldn't turn my back on family. It wasn't what my mom would want.

"See you in a few," I said.

I disconnected the call and picked up things around the living room.

"Lord, please help Brianna find a job. Father, help her find you too," I said sighing while looking at the clock.

I needed to get dressed for work, but I would wait until they got there. I was glad I finished my daily devotional and I could focus on Jack and get him off to school. He was such a sweet little boy, and I wished Brianna would take better care of him.

Seven minutes later, there was a knock at the door. I opened it and seven-year-old Jack came running in. "Aunt Addison..." He threw his arms around me with all the tightness in the world. Our relationship was great, and I was glad to be his aunt. I smiled now holding on to him just as tight.

"Hey, buddy!"

"Thanks a ton, Addi. You won't regret this and I won't forget it either," Brianna said.

If only I could to trust her, but Brianna was always tossing around excuses. Smiling and nodding, I agreed as always. "It is not a problem. Don't worry about it! Now, what job are you interviewing for?" I asked.

She shook her head. "Gotta run... no time to chat," she said. "I'll tell you all about it later. I'm late for the interview."

I frowned and yelled out to her. "God bless on the interview!"

I waved and watched her head back to her car, then turn the key, and back out of the driveway. I hoped she was telling the truth and going to an interview. I closed the door to keep the cold out.

"Hey, buddy. Want cereal?" I asked.

"Yay!" he said.

I smiled going to the kitchen where I poured him a bowl. He happily ate and even did a dance. He was such a character at times.

"You eat up. I will go finish getting ready."

"Thanks, Aunt Addison," he said and continued to eat as I rushed from the kitchen and continued to my room. I took off my robe and got dressed. When I was going to the bathroom to put my makeup on I heard a loud crash. I rushed out of my room and into the kitchen. There he was, knelt down on the floor picking up the shattered bowl my mother had gotten me.

"Are you all right?" I asked.

"I'm sorry Aunt Addison," he said. When he looked up, he had tears in his eyes. "Mommy says I can be such a klutz."

My heart tore for my nephew. I rushed to his side and stopped him from worrying about the spilled cereal on the floor.

"It's all right. It happens to everyone. You sit up there and I'll take care of everything, okay?"

He sobbed and nodded, but still looked like he was expecting me to ream him for making a mess. I didn't want Jack to worry about such frivolity. I got the mess cleaned up and looked at him as I tossed the broken bowl in the trash. "See... there's no use in crying."

He nodded and a small smile peaked on his lips. Then, he sat at the kitchen table, looking worried about whether he should even move.

"You need more? Or, did you get enough to eat?" I asked.

"I'm fine!" he said.

I frowned. I wasn't the expert on kids as, I had none, but I was certain they shouldn't go through life like this.

"I have to finish up and I'll be ready to take you to school."

I was running out of time and I needed to apply makeup quick fast and in a hurry. When I got back to the kitchen, Jack already had his coat back on and was ready and standing with his backpack in his hand.

"You're eager to get to school," I said with a laugh.

He shrugged. "Didn't want to keep you."

I tilted my head. Jack was talking way over his head. He wasn't talking like a little boy. He was talking like an old man.

"All right, little buddy. Let's get out of here."

I grabbed my purse and keys and we headed out the door. The whole way to the school, Jack remained quiet in the backseat. I peered at him through the rearview mirror and found him staring out the window.

"What are you thinking about back there?" I asked.

He looked up and his gaze met mine. "Just thinking..." He hesitated for a minute until he looked at me. "Is mom going to pick me up, or are you?" he asked. He quirked up an eyebrow, giving me an inquisitive look.

We hadn't discussed it, but I assumed that Brianna would pick him up. "Well, I'm guessing your mom will," I replied, leaving it vaguer than anything.

He smiled. "Okay."

I drove the rest of the way to his school in silence. While driving, I was thinking about how I wanted to protect him from any worry. He's young and worries so much worry for his age.

I turned into the school parking lot and followed a trail of cars around the front of the school. When I got up to the curb, I stopped the car and turned to him.

"You have everything?" I asked.

He nodded. "Thanks, Aunt Addison."

"You're welcome, buddy. Have a good day at school. I love you."

He smiled, his eyes lighting up more than before. "Love you too."

Jack waved while getting out of the car. He shut the door behind him and I watched him head towards the doors of the school. He didn't talk to anyone as he made his way inside, but that was his style. He was a shy boy and there wasn't anything wrong with it, but I worried that maybe he wasn't getting much socialization.

Jack disappeared from the school and I pulled away. I needed to get to work and try my best to concentrate. I wanted everything to be all right with Brianna and Jack as they were my only family members.

"Lord, help my family but most of all help my nephew Jack."

# CHAPTER 2

*I* browsed through pages of homes in the real estate database, hunting for the perfect home for two of my newest clients. Working as a realtor, I found it to be somewhat lucrative, but I was still praying and hoping for that big break. As I was taking notes on a potential home to show my clients, my cell phone rang. I looked over at it and saw my sister, Brianna's name across the screen. I glanced at the clock on my computer to see what time it was. It was after two o'clock.

I picked it up. "Hello?"

"Hey, Addi, it's me," she said.

"Hey... what's up? How's the job hunting going? More so, how did the interview go?" I continued to write the information for the home I would show to my client. I heard her heave a sigh on the other end of the line. I knew what that meant.

"Not great!" she said. "This time of year makes it hard to find a job. A lot of places aren't hiring and the ones that are, aren't worth anything. It's either warehouse or retail jobs. And don't even get me started on the interview. That was a joke. Do you realize they want me to work twice as hard and get paid half as much as most places out there?" She laughed. "It's all a joke!"

I groaned because it didn't sound like she was trying all that hard. "Sometimes you have to work for what they're willing to pay. It all pans out. You believe and have faith."

Brianna snickered on the other end of the line. "I'm not you, sis. I can't just have faith and believe it will all work out, but I suppose you can have all the faith for the both of us."

I didn't like that response, but she was stubborn and it would be pointless to convince her otherwise. "All right then. So, what's going on?" I asked.

"I need you to pick Jack up today. I will keep hitting the pavement and get my resume out there."

I couldn't stop her from doing that because I wanted her to find a job. "No problem," I said, even though picking Jack up meant I needed to move some of my scheduled meetings around again. "Do you want me to bring him home afterward?" I asked.

"Well, feed him first, and then you can bring him home."

"Okay, I'll do that then," I said.

We said our goodbyes, and I hung up the phone. I needed to change my schedule, to make sure I was free to get him from school at three thirty. At three ten I hurried out the door to make sure I wasn't late. After several minutes of being at the school, Jack came walking out. He looked at the cars and his eyes locked on mine. He walked towards me with his head almost down. I could tell it disappointed him that his mother wasn't here to pick him up.

"Hey, how was your day?" I asked.

"Fine!" he said. "Where's mom?" I figured he would ask that.

"Well, I'm sorry that you're stuck with me, but your mom had to run a few errands. I will feed you and then take you home."

He nodded, and a smile poked at his lips. As we drove away from the school, we talked about where he wanted to go eat. We wound up at the small diner a few blocks from his house. As soon as we settled inside, I looked through the menu. I rattled off potential things he could eat.

He settled on the mini-corn dogs and I got the turkey burger basket. After the waitress walked away, I struck up a conversation. "So, how's second grade treating you?" I asked.

He shrugged. "Fine, I suppose."

"Do you have a girlfriend?" I asked.

That got him to laughing, and I smiled at his jovial appearance. "Aunt Addison, I'm only seven."

I shrugged. "Men start at younger ages nowadays." We laughed a little more, and I continued. "How about friends? Do you have any good friends you hang out with?"

He pondered over that, a confused facial expression cast on his face. "Joe and Freddy are my friends," he said.

I smiled. "Well, that's good to hear." The waitress brought us out our food, and we ate. "What's your favorite part of school?" I asked him. "Do you have a favorite subject?"

He ate a fry and thought about it and nodded. "I like gym class."

That was an interesting choice I thought. "Really? What's your favorite part of your gym class?" I asked.

"I like to run and both Joe and Freddy are in my class." His eyes lit up. "We will be on the basketball team. Practice starts tomorrow. I'm excited about that."

"Wow! I can see you are. Can I come to your games?"

He snickered. "Of course you can." He then sat back, and we continued to eat, while he talked more about how he was looking forward to being on the team. Hearing this made me believe everything would be all right with him.

When we got done eating, I paid the tab, and we left the diner. Once we got to his house, I noticed Brianna's car wasn't out front. Jack noticed it too.

"Mom isn't home," he said.

"That's okay, buddy. Let's get you started on your homework. She'll be home soon," I said.

I parked the car in front of the house and we got out. I found the key to the house on my keyring opened the door. Once inside, Jack dropped his coat off at the closet and then went into the kitchen with his bag. He sat down at the table and worked on his homework. I didn't even have to ask him to start it.

I took my coat off and laid it on the arm of the couch and then headed into the kitchen. "Need any help?" I asked, taking the seat beside him.

"Maybe with math," he said. He pulled out his math homework, and I looked it over. After thinking about it for a second, I realized that seven-year-old math was a lot more difficult than I expected. After a while, I figured it out. I shook my head at this common core math. It made no sense.

While we worked on his homework, I heard the back door open. Brianna was home. I looked up and smiled. "Hey, sis!"

She glanced in our direction with a sad face. Her eyes narrowed as she looked at us. "Hey!"

I stood up from the table. "Jack is working on his homework and I fed him." I then lowered my voice. "How did it go with job hunting?"

She looked at me and groaned. "Don't even ask." That wasn't a great sign.

"Guess I'll get out of your hair then," I said knowing she wasn't going to elaborate. I walked over to Jack and kissed him on the head. "Goodbye, buddy! See you later."

"Bye Aunt Addison," he said.

Brianna walked me to the front door, and I turned to her. She looked worn out, and it worried me. If I would have asked about it, she would give me a hard luck story, so I didn't. "Do you need me tomorrow?" I asked.

She shook her head. "I should have it under control, but thanks."

"Okay, no problem. See you later." I waved to her and headed out the door. When I got back to my car, she had already gone back inside and was out of sight. I frowned. I didn't know what I could do to help her, but I had to pray for her and hope that everything would work out soon enough.

❄

*W*hen I got home, I couldn't believe how quiet it was. The quietness of my home overcame me and I heaved a sigh of sadness. I felt the need to write an entry in the journal to my future husband just to feel less lonely. I needed to share all the memories I had today. So, I grabbed my journal and took a seat on my couch. As the silence lingered, I wrote out my entry:

*Dear Future Husband,*

*Today was a weird day. I feel it is difficult to not have someone to come home to. I don't know why but today wasn't easy for me. I feel this way because it's the holidays and there's no one to share it with. I'm sure you know how that feels. I'm in this quiet house and I need a family to fill it. I hope and pray God brings us together soon.*

*Sometimes I sit home at night and wonder about you. I wonder if you are at home doing the same thing. I can almost imagine the person you would be. I see you as strong, confident, and loving. I need and want you in my life now. I'm trusting that one day God will bring you into my life, fulfilling all my dreams and helping me on rough days like these.*

*Things are rough because of Brianna and Jack. I love my nephew and I love my sister and I would do anything for either one of them, but she makes things so difficult. She's in the middle of looking for a job to support them, yet I feel she would much rather make excuses. She isn't the woman that our mother raised us to be and I need to believe she would soon come around.*

*I wish you were here to walk with me through this, but one day soon I will no longer walk alone. You will be my everything and I will be yours. My heart already knows you are an amazing man and I can't wait to meet you. I will sign off tonight, with the hopes and desires you will be here soon. The Lord has laid upon my heart you will come into my life in just a matter of time.*

*Forever and always,*

*Addison*

I turned to the next page in the journal and laid my hand upon the page. I took a deep breath in and wrote a prayer, bringing a sensation and a knowing within me that God was listening. It was great to write letters to my future husband, but it was even better for me to talk and pray to my heavenly Father.

*Father,*

*Thank you for today. Even though it was a rough day of seeing my nephew in such sadness, I know you have everything under control. I know that you have great plans for him. You have thoughts of peace and not of evil, to give him a future and a hope. So, I ask this day for you to guide and lead him and be there for him. Show up strong in his life. Show him Your love.*

*I also pray that Brianna wakes up and sees this beautiful child in front of her. Please help her remove whatever hindrances or obstacles in her life. Help her be the best mother she can be.*

*Father, I ask that you help her see who she is in You. I pray for her salvation even now, Lord. I pray she will accept You and that You will live in and with her. I pray that she will reach out to You and experience the breath of life! Test its length! Plumb the depths! Rise to the heights! Live a full life, full in the fullness of You.*

*I also pray for my future husband. I thank you once again for sending him. Thank you for sending a man that will love and help Jack be the man You have called him to be.*

*In Jesus' Name, Amen.*

I smiled, closing the journal knowing what I had prayed for would come to pass. It would all work out. I would see God move in every area of my life and the lives of my family and future family soon.

# CHAPTER 3

*W*aking up the next morning, I once again went through my prayer devotional. When I finished, I half-expected another call from Brianna. She would sometimes call to see if she could once again, drop off Jack for me to take him to school. However, that call never came, and I wound up feeling confident she could get Jack off to school on her own.

I got dressed for work and headed to the office. The day was a busy one. I met clients and went through several homes with them. Today, things were going pretty normal. I expected I would make it through the day without interruption, but then I got the call. I was showing a couple a home when I saw Brianna's number pop up on my cell phone.

"You continue to look through the house and I'll take this call. I'll be back in a minute," I said.

I figured another crisis came up, and I needed to get Jack from school.

"Hello?" I said, answering the call as I stepped into the other room.

"Addi?" She was crying on the other end. I heard her sniffling before she even said my name.

"Bri? What's wrong?" I asked. My heart skipped a beat as I questioned why Brianna would call crying on the other end of the line.

She sniffled into the phone. "I can't do it," she said. "I just can't do it."

She sounded depressed, and that heightened my worry. "You can't do what?" I asked. "Is Jack all right? Is he at school?"

"Yes... he's at school," she said, taking in a deep breath with her response. "But I can't be his mom. I can't be the mom he deserves to have." Her words came out, and I listened to them, trying to fathom what she could mean by it all. "I need to be out of it."

"Brianna... what are you talking about? Out of what?" I hissed. "You are his mother and you can't do anything about that. You're a good mom. Sure you're going through some troubling times, but Bri, you can't be thinking this way. Jack needs a mother and you are the only mother he has. He loves you."

There was a long hesitation. I waited for her next words. "He needs you!" She said the words, but I was certain she didn't mean them.

"What?" I asked, squealing into the phone. I then remembered the couple and lowered my voice. "You aren't thinking straight. He is your son. He's seven years old, and he needs his mother. You can't erase that or forget about him. Don't back out on him. He doesn't deserve that."

Brianna's voice shook when she spoke again. She was still crying, almost sobbing now.

"You're right. He doesn't deserve this but you're so good with him. I see the way he looks at you. I see the way he cares about you and feels so safe when you're around."

"Stop it, Brianna! You're talking crazy now."

"It is better for him to stay with you. Take good care of him. I'm sorry."

The phone went dead, and I stood there. "Brianna? Brianna?" I hissed into the phone, but she already clicked off. I pulled the phone from my ear and called her back. It went straight to voicemail, so I left a message. "Brianna, do not do this. I get that you're scared, but we'll get through this. Where are you going to go? What are you going to do? Please... just call me back." I disconnected the call and stood there for a minute. I was in disbelief. Was this happening? I called her back again, but as I dialed her number, I heard my name.

"Addison? We're ready to put an offer on the house."

I turned around to see Mr. Waverley standing at the living room entrance. I forced a smile like nothing had happened. "Great! I'll get the offer sent in right away. Let's discuss this."

My mind was racing, and I was thinking about Brianna. How could she do this? I thought.

❄

*A*s the cars cleared out in front of me, I continued to wait for Jack. I didn't know how to tell him why his mother wasn't there to pick him up, but I knew I needed to be upfront with him. I saw him come out of the building and his eyes went to my car. His head fell as he walked to the car.

He opened the back door sliding into the car, then shut the door behind him. "Mom's busy?" he asked.

I glanced in the rearview mirror and nodded. "Sorry, buddy."

He shrugged. "It is fine." He then looked up at me again. "I have my first basketball practice tonight. Will you bring me back?" he asked.

"Of course. When is it?" I asked.

"Five," he answered. He turned looking back out the window. I watched him for a minute before turning back around and heading away from the curb. We didn't have a lot of time to grab food.

When we got to Jack's favorite restaurant, he didn't even perk up. We ordered and then when we sat down, I could tell that he was thinking way too hard about things. "You want to talk about it?" I asked.

He looked at me and nodded. "Is mommy all right?" he asked. His voice was quiet as he stared at me, looking long and hard to see if I would tell him the truth.

I glanced at him. "Well, I will be honest with you," I said. He listened as I tried to give him the condensed version of what was going on. "Your mommy asked me if I could watch over you for a while. She has things going on and she thinks you'll be better off staying with me." I paused and asked. "What do you think of that?"

He scrunched up his nose, then shrugged. "For how long?" he asked.

That was an obvious question one would ask, but I didn't know the answer to it. "I'm not sure buddy," I admitted. "Could be days or a few weeks."

When his eyes widened, I reached out and touched his hand. His eyes met mine. "I have always loved you as if you were my own. You know that, right?"

He nodded.

"You won't go without and I won't leave you," I continued. "Just trust me and we will get through this together. Okay?"

He nodded, and the waitress arrived back with our food. We went on eating, with neither one of us saying much of anything. I continued to watch him because I wanted to believe he knew he could count on me.

We got done eating and left the restaurant. It was time for basketball practice. Since it was his first practice, and I wasn't even sure what it entailed, I parked in the lot next to the gym. We got out of the car and headed through the double doors. I opened the door for him and he walked in, not looking the least bit nervous.

The minute we got in the gymnasium, I saw about twenty kids milling around. At least twenty parents stood around waiting and wanting to know what was going on. It appeared to be mass chaos, but I looked around the gym and spotted a very handsome man standing with a clipboard. He had a whistle around his neck and I know I shouldn't be thinking this way but he was very attractive. He was writing something down on his notepad looking unfazed because the surrounding noise was growing.

So, Jack and I headed over to him. When I reached him, he didn't look up. I cleared my throat, expecting that to cause him to look up. Instead, he told me where to go. He didn't even acknowledge me.

"Child over there... parents over there." That was all he said, pointing as he motioned for us to disperse.

I frowned. It was very unprofessional. I didn't think it would cause too many issues if he would just look up and acknowledge us. I cleared my throat again. "Excuse me, but I have a question."

He sighed and looked up and his demeanor changed. "Oh, hey... I'm sorry. It's hectic being the first practice of the year. I'm new to this. The first day, you know. How can I help you?" He put on a charming smile that would make any woman melt and ignored his clipboard.

I smiled back even though it was lazy. "I was just wondering how this evening works," I said. "Am I supposed to stay? How long does it last?"

"You're more than welcome to stay and watch your son," he started.

I blushed and looked down at Jack. He looked around at the rest of the kids, seeking his friends. "He's my nephew," I corrected, then looked back at the man.

The man straightened up and seemed a different person than the one we first encountered. Something caught his attention and there was a sparkle in his eyes. I placed the loose hair on my face behind my ear. I don't know why I was getting so nervous. Was I now blushing too? What was this?

# CHAPTER 4

"The name's Isaac. I'm the new basketball coach." He stretched out his hand and I grabbed it. I shook his hand, then pulled my hand away. "The practice will last an hour. It is up to you whether you stay, but it's nice if for the first practice all family members stick around. There's no pressure to stay around though if you have other things to do."

He smiled again, revealing his bright white teeth. He had a nice smile.

I nodded. "Then I'll stick around. Thanks."

I turned to Jack, and he spotted his friends and wanted to rush off to them. I nodded and laughed as he went off, leaving me alone. I looked back at Isaac and he was laughing too.

"Thank you!" I said again.

I turned around and headed away from him. My focus was now on Jack and how fast things changed. I sat down in the bleachers as others took their seats. On the court, the kids all formed in a group as Isaac went over to them and talked. I was watching Jack, praying he would listen and not get too engrossed in talking to his friends. To my relief, he turned his attention to the coach. I breathed a sigh of relief as Isaac talked to them and Jack paid attention.

After about ten minutes in what I would call a huddle, he broke from the group and took his place in the middle of the court. He then spoke to the parents and other adults were in the audience.

"Hello and thank you all for coming out today for the first practice."

I kept my eyes on Jack and he was still watching Isaac. When I turned my attention back to him, I noticed that Isaac's eyes were on me now. When our eyes met, I blushed, because he was staring at me in a way that confused me. I looked away from him, only because I didn't expect to blush again.

He continued to talk. "It's the parents and guardians that make all of this possible and I am indebted to each of you."

When I looked back at him, he was no longer staring at me. I took a deep breath and refocused my breathing.

"So, tonight's practice will be the basketball basics. Think of it as basketball 101. If you have questions for me, then you are free to stay after and ask me anything." He shot a winning smile towards us. "Thank you so much."

He turned away from us and went back to the kids. I took my eyes back to Jack, trying not to dwell on the fact that a few minutes earlier, our eyes met. I couldn't believe he was making me blush once again. It was a feeling I wasn't used to. It was a feeling I hadn't had in a long time.

As I watched the kids interacting with him, they did drills and I was rooting for Jack, even if it was mentally. I didn't even notice when someone took a seat next to me until she talked.

"Which one is yours?" she asked.

I turned to her and smiled, then pointed to Jack. "He's my nephew Jack."

She smiled. "My son, Brad will be the star on this team. He's been playing basketball since he was three years old."

I nodded. "Wow... three... impressive." I could tell she was one mother that would brag about her son and I couldn't blame her. I could see myself as one of those doting parents. "Which one is your son?" I asked.

She pointed him out and I had to admit that he was running circles around many of the others, including Jack. But he was also four inches taller than the rest of the clan.

I smiled. "Looking good," I said.

The woman nodded and then we went back to looking at the practice. Then she talked again. "So, it's your nephew you say?" she asked.

I watched Jack before glancing at the woman beside me. "Yeah, his mom is busy working, so I'm doing a favor."

I hated lying about it, but I didn't want to get into the mix of answering any more questions. She smiled and turned back to the kids and I breathed a sigh of relief because I didn't have to dive into anymore awkwardness.

The rest of the hour went by and the doting mother that sat beside me didn't speak up much. The only time she spoke up was for the occasional, good shot, that was a close call, or that's too bad when Jack missed his shot.

When practice was over, there was a lot of scurrying around of parents grabbing their kids. It was like they were seeing who could get out of the gym the fastest. I walked up to Jack, and he looked a little disappointed, so I wanted to cheer him up.

"That was a good practice," I said.

He looked up, giving me a weak smile. "I'm awful," he said.

I shook my head. "No, you're not bad. It's just some of these kids have been playing for a while now. You weren't bad and you'll only get better."

He didn't seem all that convinced as we headed towards the door. When I heard Isaac's voice calling out to us I stopped. "Jack's Aunt," he called. I slowly turned around and saw he was approaching us at a quick speed. He looked a tad embarrassed. "I'm sorry, I didn't catch your name."

"It's Addison," she said. "May I help you with something?" I asked.

"Um yeah..." He looked around. He was acting nervous, but I cast a look at Jack and saw he wasn't interested in standing there. "I was going to suggest that maybe Jack would want to come here and have extra practice time. I mean, some of these boys are more advanced and I don't want Jack to feel left behind. He has potential."

I smiled. That was nice of him to offer. I glanced down at Jack. "What do you say?" He nodded slightly and his face shined with a touch of happiness. I looked back up at Isaac. "Thanks for the offer. It is very nice of you to do this."

His grin was bright. "Of course!" Then hesitated for a moment before asking, "Would you be the one to bring him to practices?"

"Well, I uh..." I stammered for a minute, before catching my footing. "I suppose we shall see," I responded with some uneasiness. "But for right now... yes."

I thought his eyes lit up at the mention of that, but I couldn't be too sure.

"Okay... then how about you coming back tomorrow at six?"

"That would be great. Thanks!"

He waved to us as we turned and headed out of the gym. I found it interesting that this coach would be so interested in how well Jack did or didn't do. It intrigued me, because anyone that took a liking to Jack, was someone I would be drawn to.

"Did you have fun?" I asked him as we walked to my car.

"You bet," he said.

And that's all I needed to hear. The rest would work itself out. I was sure of that.

❄

*I* leaned over and kissed Jack on the forehead. "Goodnight buddy," I said.

"Goodnight Aunt Addison," he answered back. He rolled onto his side and I slipped out of the spare room. Once in the hall, I pondered over what this would mean for him and what this would mean for me.

On the way home from the gym, we swung by his place and his mom wasn't there. I had hoped that I would run into Brianna and talk some sense into her. But it wasn't meant to be. We grabbed clothes that would keep him for a week, but there was no guarantee she would be back even by then. I was flying blind and didn't know what all this would entail.

When we got back to my house, I dialed up Brianna's number while Jack went to his new room to play his video game. Not to my surprise, the call went straight to voicemail.

"You've reached my voicemail. You know what to do." Then there was a beep, and I left a message.

"Bri... I don't know what to say, other than you're making a huge mistake. This isn't what you want to do. I know you and you love Jack. You need to come home and make things right. I'll help you, but I can't do that if I don't even know where you are. So, please... call me and we'll get through this."

I disconnected the call and felt a huge weight on my chest. What would happen if she never called back? I didn't want to find out. I got up and went over to my journal. I pulled it from the shelf and went back over to my favorite comfy chair and sat down.

I opened it up to the next blank page and sat there for a moment, contemplating what I wanted to write to him this evening. As the thoughts danced through my mind, I wrote my journal entry:

*Dear Future Husband,*

*Today has been quite the day. I still can't wrap my head around the fact that Brianna just up and left. I would do anything for Jack, you know this, but my sister isn't thinking straight. She is going about this the wrong way and how can I tell Jack that his mother might never come back? How can I stand here and willingly know I might never see my sister again?*

*Our mom would be so disappointed in her and I want God to help her through this, but I also want to know what I can do to help her. I wish you were here with me my dear husband because you would know what to say to help me understand. I need your strong arms to comfort me in these times, but I will give Jack the loving home he deserves. For as long as he needs me, I will be there for him. It may not be easy, but it's what we do for our families.*

*I don't know how to be a mother to him, but I will give him all the love I have. I will make sure he feels loved and cared for. Tonight he started basketball and the look on his face is priceless. I can tell that he loves the sport, but he needs someone to believe in him. I will be that someone.*

*I will not let Jack down, I will not let our mother down, and I won't let myself down. Until we meet my dear husband, I want you to know I am still fighting for the moment we lay eyes on one another. That day will be a dream come true. I will remember it always when it happens.*

*Forever and always,*

*Addison*

I closed the journal and leaned back in the rocking chair. "Forever and always, my dear husband. We will find our way to each other."

# CHAPTER 5

*I* wanted to give Brianna the benefit of the doubt. In my mind, she needed a day to figure out what she wanted and then she would come around. However, the next day I took Jack to school and picked him up and still... no call from Brianna. I attempted to call her while I was at work, but she still wouldn't respond to any of my voicemails.

Jack said nothing about it, but I could sense he was thinking about where his mother was. I was glad basketball was in his life right now because it would help keep his mind off his mother leaving.

I took him back to the school for his private practice with Isaac. I knew he couldn't wait to hit the floor.

"Are you excited about getting back on the court?" I asked him.

He smiled and nodded. "I love playing basketball."

I reached down and took his hand in mind and we headed to the school. When we got to the gymnasium, Isaac was there, and he was shooting baskets. I stopped and gazed at him, caught by the form of his body. His muscles were visible beneath the sleeves of his t-shirt. He didn't even notice we were standing there and watching him.

Jack's voice caught me off guard. "Whoa..." he said. I shot him a look, then saw he was watching Isaac as one after one, he was making the baskets. "He's good."

I smiled and turned back to the man before us. Jack was right. He was a great basketball player, and his kind nature was only the tip of the iceberg of who this man was. Jack and I moved closer to him and I cleared my throat, not wanting to interrupt him. That was the one basket he missed as he quickly turned around to look at us. His face lit up.

"Addison... Jack... I'm glad you both made it," he said. He reached out to shake my hand. I took it in my grasp. His handshake was strong.

"We appreciate you offering this," I stated as I let the handshake fade away. "I know, for one, that Jack is super excited to get started."

He nodded and looked down at him. "Then let's not waste another minute." Isaac grabbed a basketball and tossed it to Jack. Jack smiled with a sheepish grin. He took his coat off and handed it to me, then turned back to his coach. I fell back and took a seat on the bleachers and watched the private practice ensue.

It started off with Jack throwing free throws and Isaac observing him. Then Isaac would stop watching and help Jack with his form. After fifteen minutes, Jack actually made a few of the baskets. Each basket made would have him high-fiving Isaac. Then, Isaac would look my way and grin, giving me encouragement along the way. At one point, Isaac looked at me and winked in my direction. I got a funny feeling that had me hopeful, but I wasn't used to that feeling and I tried to push it away. This was about Jack learning to play a game that he loved and that was all. But I couldn't forget the feeling that Isaac gave me when he looked at me. The feeling was warm, sincere, and gentle. It was what I'd desired to have in my life. Then, again, I had to force those thoughts away, because it was all the wrong timing.

Practice went on for over an hour and by the end of it, Jack looked exhausted, but he was still smiling. I walked over to them, ready to thank Isaac for making Jack forget about the loss he was feeling. But, I didn't want to go into that with him. It was still too early. So, I put on a smile and while Jack put on his coat, I looked at Isaac. "You are a great coach," I said.

A wide smile appeared on his face. "It's the kids that make me a good coach," he said. "I'm happy to be here and I'll tell you this... Jack has so much potential, so I would love to continue to work with him. He takes directions well and I can sense he'll approve over time and before you know it, he'll be the star of the team."

I laughed and looked at Jack. Seeing his face light up, was enough for me to endorse Isaac's coaching abilities. "We'll keep coming, as long as you're still offering," I said. I met his gaze, and he nodded.

"Then I'll see you tomorrow for another practice and Friday there's a normal practice. I'm sure all the kids will be impressed by Jack's skills." He turned to Jack. "Isn't that right, buddy?" They high-fived again, and I chuckled. It was a sweet exchange, and he called him buddy just like I did.

"All righty then. We'll see you tomorrow." I turned to him, thanked him again, and Jack and I headed towards the gymnasium door. I knew it was probably my imagination, but as we left, I felt like Isaac's eyes were still on us, but I didn't dare bother to look.

❄

*I*t was a busy day on Thursday at work. I kept glancing at my work and the clock, just to make sure I didn't lose track of time to pick Jack up. That was by far the biggest change, having to remind myself that I couldn't work as late as I normally would have. I had new responsibilities that were sure to change up my life.

I was about to leave the office when I heard my phone ringing at my desk. I rushed to pick it up. "This is Addison Baker."

"Hello, Ms. Baker. This is Lily Montoya. I work for Braxton Washington, CEO, and owner of Washington Industries. Not sure if you've heard of him or the company. Anyway, we are a big conglomerate that's in the midst of seeking out some land for new office space. And Mr. Washington has heard good things about you, so he was hoping to meet up and look at obtaining your services."

My mouth dropped open, the minute she said who she was and who she was calling for. Of course, I knew who he was. Everyone knew about Washington Industries. "Um... yeah... I know who he is and I would love to speak with him. I know of some great land that would interest him." Having them as a client would mean I had made it big in the real estate business. It would be an answer to my prayers. I would do anything to take that on.

"Great! I know it is short notice, but would you be able to meet up this afternoon still?"

"Of course!" I said, then it hit me that that wasn't possible. I had to pick up Jack and take him to practice. "Oh wait a minute... I just remembered I won't be able to do that. I could do tomorrow."

"Well, tomorrow his schedule is pretty busy. I could check with him to see if he could do something like six thirty."

I fell back into my seat. That would mean I couldn't get Jack to his basketball practice. "Well, I'm not sure if that would work. Can I call you back tomorrow?" I asked.

"Yes... you can. I must warn you though, Mr. Washington wants to be very fast on this. He's not a patient man."

"I understand," I quietly stated. She rattled off the phone number where I could reach her and I promised to call back in the morning. I hung up the call and sat there for a moment in a daze. It was already starting where I was seeing how difficult it would be to take on Jack and maintain my job. I was so engrossed in thinking about it all that I barely noticed I was almost late to pick up Jack from school.

I quickly stood up, grabbed my purse and dashed out of the office.

I was glad that traffic was light. I made it to the school in record time, but, Jack was already outside and leaning against the tree as he waited for me. When I pulled up in the line, there were like ten cars ahead of me. As I waited, I watched him. While I inched up through the line, I saw some boy come over to him and start to talk to him. He looked angrily at Jack, said a few things, then turned around in a huff and stormed off. Or, at least, that's how I read it, without knowing what was going on.

Jack looked towards the vehicle and walked out to me, then got in the backseat. I was quick to inquire about it. "Hey, what'd that kid want?" I asked.

I glanced through the rearview mirror and he looked hesitant to talk about it. "Oh... it's nothing. He just wanted to talk about something stupid."

I immediately didn't buy that, but I frowned and didn't know if I should press on. I didn't know what was and wasn't appropriate for me to say in that moment. I looked back to the front and pulled away from the curb, knowing I needed to come back to it.

As we drove back to the house, I inquired about basketball. "You want to continue going to basketball practice, right?"

He laughed in the back seat. "Yeah... of course," he said.

"Okay then. I was making sure." I didn't want to sway him away from it because he had to be missing his mom. This was one thing that could get his mind in a different direction. But, I wondered the whole time how could I have it all.

When we got home, we ate supper and then he worked on homework. He said he didn't have much and worked on one worksheet and then it was time to go back to the school for practice. Again, when we got in there, Isaac was practicing his own baskets. This time, he sensed our presence and stopped before I could clear my throat.

He turned back to us and still held that same smile that was so wide and bright. "Hey you two," he said. "How are you doing this fine evening?"

I couldn't even fake a smile as I said that I was doing fine. There was something about him that made me smile big and wide.

"I'm doing good," Jack said.

"Good to hear buddy," he said.

"Hey, want to head into the locker room? I have some new jerseys that came in and you can try yours on."

"Yeah!" he said excitedly. He ran off to the locker room, without even saying goodbye.

I smiled as I watched him go off. "How are you really doing, Addison?" he asked.

I turned to him, surprised by the question. "Oh... I'm doing all right," I said. I didn't know him all that well and didn't want to burden him with my problems.

"Are you?" he asked. "You seem a little different today." He shrugged. "I'm a good listener." He then paused. "I mean, I don't want to pry or anything. I don't know what your situation is like, but I do know you're the one that is always here with Jack. You both seem to have a good bond." He smiled. "It is none of my business. I'm making sure that everything is all right, you know."

I wasn't used to someone being concerned about how I was doing and it was nice. "It's a rough time right now," I admitted. "I'm looking after Jack for a while and I have this job that requires a lot of time. I have an important meeting that I should take tomorrow evening at six thirty, but Jack has practice. I don't want to let him down but I do need this deal. I have an extra mouth to feed and take care of."

I couldn't even control the words from falling out of my mouth. I quickly snapped my mouth shut.

"Wow... that was probably more than you wanted to know." I laughed. "I'm sorry. I tend to get overly excited and spill my thoughts. Please, don't mind me."

He was right though. He was a great listener because he did listen to me and didn't interrupt my thoughts. When I finished, he smiled.

"Don't ever apologize for being who you are, Addison." He then scrunched up his face in thought. "I have an idea. Would it help if you dropped Jack off at practice, go to the meeting, and then come back to get him?"

I shrugged. "I'm not sure when the meeting would be over and practice only goes to seven."

He laughed. "Well, I know this might come as a shock to you because you don't know me all that well. I wouldn't leave Jack by himself if you weren't here. I can watch him a little longer. Put him through a few extra drills, you know. If you have an important meeting, you should be there."

"That's really nice," I finally conceded. "I would appreciate that."

He nodded. "Then it's settled."

We heard Jack coming out of the locker room, and we turned our attention to him. He came running out, looking like a true professional.

"Whoa buddy, you look great!" he said.

Isaac shot a look my way, then winked at me, and then focused all his attention back to Jack. How could one man be so sweet? I thought as I fell back and took my seat. But in mind, Isaac was the dream man and Jack and I was both lucky to have met him earlier that week. I was very appreciative, and I didn't know how I would ever repay him.

# CHAPTER 6

*J*ust when I thought everything was going to go my way, I
got a phone call that changed everything. It left me so
confused. It came at two o'clock in the afternoon on
Friday. I answered my cell phone, not recognizing the number.

"Hello?" I answered.

"Hello... is this Addison Baker?"

"Yes, this is she."

"Hello, Addison, this is Principal Birkman at Trentmoor Elementary School."

My heart sunk into my stomach. I was getting a call from the Principal and I figured it wasn't good.

"Hello, Principal Birkman, how may I help you?" I stopped doing any work, so I could listen to the call.

"I'm calling because I want to reach out and discuss something that is bothering me about your nephew Jack. Do you have a few minutes to talk on Monday?" he asked.

"Um... can you give me a hint?" I asked.

"I would rather discuss it with you in person. I'm not free anymore this afternoon, so I thought maybe Monday morning we could speak."
I looked at my calendar of meetings with clients I had going on

Monday. I had to meet with him, which was far more important than anything else.

"What time? I'll work it into my schedule," I said.

"We could meet at eight o'clock if that would work, right after you drop him off here."

"Okay. I'll be there." I wrote it down on my calendar and we said goodbye. I heaved a sigh as I thought about it. I knew that I would have to dwell on it the entire weekend and I wasn't looking forward to that.

When it was time to get him from school, I made it there so I was the first one in line. When he got in the car, I decided we needed to have a heart to heart. As I drove away from the curb, I started that conversation.

"Hey, bud, I need to talk to you," I started.

"Am I in trouble?" he quickly asked.

He couldn't be in trouble until I knew exactly what was going on. "Not really," I stated. "I have a few things I want to discuss with you. Is there anything you want to talk about? I know this has been a tough week for you. Maybe, I've been a bit preoccupied with everything to ask certain questions. You can talk to me about anything. You know that, right?"

"Yeah... I know that," he quietly stated. The backseat then went quiet. I continued to drive, heading towards the house as I waited for him to go on. It wasn't until I turned onto my street that he continued. "I miss mom," he said.

"I know, buddy, so do I." I turned into the driveway and turned the car off, but didn't make a move to get out. I turned around to look at him. His eyes met mine and there were tears behind them. "It's okay, Jack. You can talk to me."

"Did I do something to make her mad, so she would leave?" he asked.

The minute he asked, my heart broke for him. "Hon... this has nothing to do with you. You have to believe that. Your mom is working through some things, but we'll all get through it. I promise you that."

I reached out and touched his leg and he looked up and nodded. "I got a call from your Principal. Do you know what that's about?" I asked.

His eyebrows furrowed, and he shrugged. "I don't know."

I wasn't going to get any answers there, so I dropped it. "Okay. Let's get inside and get you fed. You're going to basketball practice and I have a meeting, but I'll be back as soon as I can."

We got out of the car and headed inside. There had to be a reason to get a call from the Principal. I knew that I could only sit back and wait for Monday to find out what was going on.

❄

$\mathcal{I}$ promised Isaac I would be back as soon as I could and I made sure to fulfill that promise. I went to the meeting and kept things simple by proposing my case to get their real estate deal. Braxton Washington was an assertive, but pleasurable man. I left the meeting feeling confident that I had done my best. He said I would hear back from someone at his company no later than Tuesday. Monday and Tuesday were two important days. Waiting seemed to be my life right now.

I glanced at the clock as I hurried back to the school. It was seven thirty, so I figured that was much better than it could have been. When I got back to the school, Jack wasn't throwing baskets, instead, he was on the bleachers and he was talking to Isaac. They seemed to be deep in conversation and I almost hated to interrupt them.

However, as I drew closer Isaac looked up. "And she's back," he said. He smiled and stood to his feet. Jack joined him.

"Hey, Aunt Addison," Jack said as he moved closer to me and gave me a great big hug.

"Hey, buddy. How did practice go?"

"Do you want to tell her, or should I?" Isaac asked.

Jack beamed. "I will. I shot a three-pointer and made it."

"Way to go!" I gave him a high-five, and he looked pleased with himself. "I take the practice is helping?" I turned to Isaac, and he nodded.

"Jack is a great student." He then paused as he stared at me. "Hey bud, will you do me a favor and go take those two basketballs to the locker room for me?" he asked. Jack obliged as she ran off.

I knew that was code for Isaac wanting to talk to me and I was right. "How are you doing?" he asked.

I smiled. "I'm doing all right. The meeting went great and I'm hanging in there. I have to have faith in God."

"That's good to hear," he said. He looked around the room and then back at me when he didn't see Jack coming back yet. You could tell he was nervous. "So, I'm going to ask you something. I really don't want to be too forward, but it's been a question that's been on my mind from the first moment I met you." I was nervous, especially when he put it that way.

"Go on," I said.

"Would you like to go out sometime?" he asked.

My eyes widened as I pondered his question. "You mean a date?"

He laughed. "Well, you can call it that if you want. It doesn't have to be, but I would be open for that."

He was handsome, no doubt. He was even cuter when he got nervous, such as in this moment. Every part of me wanted to say yes to him, but I couldn't. What Principal Birkman had to tell me and having to take care of Jack weighed on my mind. I couldn't get involved with him even if it was only a date.

"Well, I'm flattered that you offered, Isaac. But I don't think it's the right time. I got a call from Principal Birkman and he needs to talk to me on Monday. Something about Jack and I don't know what I'm going to do. Plus, trying to get into something relationship wise would take me away from Jack. He's my focus and priority right now. I have to make sure he is okay first. So, while it's a nice offer. I'm sorry but I have to decline."

He looked disappointed, but then comforted me. "Don't worry about Principal Birkman. He's an old softie. I'm sure it will all work out. And even if I'm disappointed, I understand."

I was grateful to hear that. Jack came back at that moment and our conversation ended. We waved to him and I gave him an extra-long look, before turning away from him. He wasn't the only one disappointed.

On the way to the car, Jack eagerly talked about his three-pointer and we discussed that. By the time he got home, he was exhausted and ready for bed.

"Go get cleaned up and I'll be up to tuck you in."

He excitedly agreed and ran up the stairs. I couldn't believe that happy boy right there, would have a reason for the Principal to call me. I went into the living room and grabbed the journal, so I could write out my entry, before tucking Jack in for the night. I sat down and opened it up to the blank page. I didn't even have to think about what I wanted to say:

*Dear Future Husband,*

*When I think things are bound to get easier, they get more complicated. Principal Birkman called me and said he needed to talk to me about Jack. I can't help but think of the many reasons that could be. But I'm holding onto the positive side of things. I'm praying to God about it and I'm hoping that it's not any of the horrible things that have run through my mind already.*

*And then there's this guy. Part of me wonders if it could be you. He's so generous, and he loves Jack. I can see it in his eyes, but I don't even know him. He asked me out on a date and oh, how I so want to go, but again... I think that maybe my life is too complicated for that. What would happen if I fell for someone and got carried away, only to be left broken? Or, on the opposite end of that spectrum, I could open my heart and find that love really does exist and that it's not some fantasy.*

*Yet, I know that things aren't right for any man to be brought into my situation. He would truly have to be the right man. I have baggage and while Jack is a wonderful boy, I can't fault anyone for being nervous about that. There are a lot changes when you have a kid to raise and it would be too much to date right now. What if we go out on a date and things don't work out? That is Jack's coach and I don't want that coaching aspect to ruin the very thing that Jack loves. I'm not in the position to bring men in and out of my life now that Jack is here. There is so many things I have to consider now with Jack in my life. So, I turned down the opportunity to go out with someone that could be a perfect match. But if it's meant to be, it will be and I will trust in that. I hope you well, dear future husband and I pray your journey is amazing and wonderful like you are.*

*Forever and always,*
  *Addison*

After signing my name I wrote a short simple prayer to God:

*Father,*

*Your will be done. Whatever you desire, I am all for it. Have your way and show me the way in everything. Give me the peace and the go-ahead when it is right to date. Help me Father to know when it is right.*

*In Jesus' Name, Amen!*

# CHAPTER 7

*A*djusting to life with a child wasn't easy for anyone, especially when it happened in the way that it did with me. It was one thing during the week when Jack would be at school and I would be at work. I didn't communicate much with him, other than taking him to practice and then working on homework. Come Saturday, it was quite a different scenario. I wondered what Jack would like to do besides basketball and forcing him to go to school.

It turned out that he was a pretty simple kid and only wanted to be entertained by television and video games. But, it wasn't exactly something I wanted him to sit around doing all day.

"How about friends that you go out and play with?" I asked. He just shrugged and continued to play his video game. I frowned at that and tried to push him to move outside of the four walls of the living room. "Do you like to draw? Read? Go to the movies? Go to the zoo?"

I was rattling off things that I thought would make him happy. All he did was shrug his shoulders and continue clicking away hard on the video game controller. When it was time to eat, I did force him to eat at the kitchen table. Then after he ate, it was right back to the television and more video game playing. I knew that his life had been uprooted in a matter of days. So, I didn't want to be the crabby Aunt that would force him to do something. I was still trying to make things stable between us, so I let him go and do what he wanted.

That was Saturday though. Come Sunday, I woke up early and felt it would be a different story. I yawned getting out of bed. Then, threw my robe on and went down to the living room and grabbed my daily devotional from its spot.

Sunday had to be my favorite day of the week. It was my time to thank God for my blessings and to spend time in His presence with other saints. And while things appeared meek and dreary, I knew that only the best would come from the situation. I needed to be patient. I opened up the devotional to give thanks to God.

*Father,*

*I lift my prayers up today for a new week and a new beginning. God, thank you for the blessings You lay upon me each day. While I know that right now, they might not be so clear, I trust that things are only going to get better if I seek out your face. Jack is still too young to know what's going on right now. Help me to give him the answers that he needs. Help me to be the role model that he deserves.*

*Give me strength as I meet with his Principal tomorrow and go over things with him. I may not know what this is about, but I will be strong enough to hear him out. Also, dear God... watch for my future husband, as you mold him to be the man that you want me to have. Also, mold me to be the woman that you want him to have. I trust that you are placing him in my life as we speak. Father, give me the willingness to know when the right one comes along.*

*I thank You for Jack and the gift you've brought into my life. Also, look out for Brianna, as she's still going through so much and I know that above anything else, she needs you.*

*I ask all these things in Your name. In Jesus' Mighty Name, Amen!*

I closed my eyes and silently gave another small prayer. I then closed the journal and got up from my spot in the living room. I dropped the devotional back off on my bookshelf and headed off to Jack's room.

I opened the door and peeked my head in, to find that as I expected, he was sound asleep after a long night of gaming. I walked over to his bed and leaned down.

"Hey, it is time to get up sleepy head." He groaned and moved about the bed, then his eyes fluttered open. "Get up! We have a busy day," I said.

I stood up and went over to his window, opening the curtain so the sun would shine in. "Ugh!" he groaned.

I laughed and shook my head. He was actually a lot like me when I was his age. Then I came to realize the importance of getting up early on Sunday and going to church. It was only a matter of time that he would too.

"It's a beautiful morning," I said. "Rise and shine!"

That got a little more movement, and he finally sat up and rubbed his eyes. "Why so early?" he asked in a groggy voice.

"Because we're going to church," I replied.

He looked at me with a bewildered look. "Momma never takes me to church," he said.

I felt a little sad to hear that, and I raised an eyebrow at his arguing face. "All the more reason we should go," I said in a soothing voice. I then gave him a smile and moved past the bed. I walked over to the closet where I put some clothes from his old home. He didn't have much to choose from, but I pulled out a pair of khaki pants and a button-up shirt and then turned to him. Sometime next week when I got the money from a deal that was a few months back, we'll definitely go shopping to get him some more clothes but for now, it was time for church.

"Get dressed and then meet me in the kitchen."

He looked over at his clothes and I left his room and went to my own. I had a little more to get done before I could head off and make breakfast, but I got to it. I grabbed a skirt and blouse from my closet and then my underwear and bra and went to the bathroom where I took a shower. Typically, I would spend a good part of the shower singing my favorite songs, but not today. I didn't want Jack to get done and wander down the kitchen before me. I made sure to finish up in record time. I then got dressed and brushed my teeth, then brushed out my hair and applied a bit of makeup.

As I headed out of my room, I heard shuffling on the stairs and knew that Jack had beat me, but only by a minute or so. I hurried down the steps and got in the kitchen. His hair was still a mess, but I would help him with that later. "Did you brush your teeth?" I asked.

He nodded and then let out a small yawn. I chuckled and started working on getting us breakfast. I was glad I had gotten some extra bacon and eggs the last time I made it to the store. I put it on and worked on that while Jack sat at the table in a stupor for looking so tired. When breakfast finished cooking, I gave him a plate and poured him a glass of milk and then we sat down together.

"Thanks," he said as he took a drink of milk.

I watched him and this sensation of love overpowered me. God gave me the gift to be able to take care of him when Brianna couldn't. I needed to accept that honor and not worry so much.

"How are your eggs?" I asked as he took his first bite.

He nodded. "Okay. I usually have them scrambled."

I hadn't even considered asking him what he preferred. I marked it up in my mind that I should remember that Jack has a right to an opinion too. "I'm sorry about that. I'll remember that next time," I said. I took a drink from my own glass. "Do you want to go to Sunday school or stay in the church service with me?" I asked him as we ate.

His eyes bugged out, and he looked nervous. "I'd rather stay with you," he said.

I nodded. "That is fine with me. I wanted to check and make sure." We had a nice children's program, but I could understand that he would be nervous since it was his first time here.

We finished eating up our breakfast, and I helped him brush his hair. Which after that, he changed the way I had brushed it, but it still looked good, so we left the house. I was glad I was able to open him up to a new experience.

❄

We pulled into the parking lot as several cars from the first service were pulling out. I grabbed one of the spots that were close to the West entrance and then we got out of the car and went towards the door. We entered and one of the Church ushers greeted us. I smiled and took a program and then entered deeper into the foyer.

Jack grabbed my hand, and we turned towards the sanctuary when I heard Jack's voice. "There's Coach Isaac," he said.

I shot a glance towards where he was pointing. Sure enough, Isaac McCabe was standing next to a stained glass window. He was talking to one of the church members that I had seen many times.

I watched him and then like he could sense my eyes on him, he turned to see us. His face lit up, but all I could do was frown. I didn't know why he would be at this church. I had never seen him there before. I glanced down at Jack as Isaac moved to us.

"Hello," he said. There was a huge grin spreading across his face.

"Coach McCabe, this is a surprise. Don't recall you being at this church before."

He grinned. "Addison... please call me Isaac," he said.

In light of him asking me out on a date and me saying no, I didn't think that was wise that.

"Coach McCabe," I said, letting him know we will keep this professional.

His eyebrow raised up and I could tell he was laughing inwardly by the expression on his face.

"Hey, little man," he said high-fiving Jack. "Good to see you."

Jack smiled, obviously not shy around his coach. "Aunt Addison can I go see Troy?" he asked. He pointed over to where Troy was standing.

"Of course, but don't run off," I said.

"I won't!" I watched as he went over to the boy and they started talking to one another. I almost forgot that Isaac was still standing near me until I felt his eyes boring two holes into me.

I turned around and blushed. "So, I'll repeat that. I don't recall seeing you here." I tilted my head, and he smiled.

"This would be the first time," he responded to that.

"Hmmm... so did you happen to find out I attend church here and decide to use the church to get to me?"

His eyes widened, a look of obvious shock on his face until he laughed lightly. "Well, no that never crossed my mind, Addison. I didn't do a massive search to see what church you go to." He chuckled again. "Truth is that I am new to the neighborhood and wanted to find a nice church to attend. I thought I'd give it a try. This is coincidental that you just happened to be here too." He paused and when I didn't acknowledge his words, he pressed on. "I promise you it's all a coincidence," he said.

I nodded, actually believing him, but thinking how crazy of a coincidence it truly was. "It's a nice church. I hope you enjoy it," I said.

"Thank you!" he said.

I met his gaze once more and was going to excuse myself when I saw Jack coming back up to me. "Hey... can I go to Sunday school with Troy?" he asked.

My mouth hung down slightly as I didn't expect that he would appear so excited about it. It was great to know that he could have friends here already and wasn't going to feel so timid about it.

I nodded. "Have fun!"

"Thanks!" He then hurried off to his friend, and I looked to see that Isaac was looking at me again.

"Well, I guess I'll see you around," I said.

"That you will," he replied.

I left him and went into the sanctuary where I greeted a couple more greeters. Then, I took a seat in the back of the sanctuary. I was only there for a couple minutes when I spotted Isaac scooting in the same row I was in. His eyes met mine, and I had to admire his determination. I scooted over, so he would have more room, and then he took the spot next to me. There was one thing that he had going for him at the moment and that was that he was a church-goer. I couldn't deny he was a step ahead of other men, but I still had way too much going on. There was so much on my mind than to think about him as anything more than a nice man. Jack and work were all I could focus on right now. Adding a relationship would only complicate things. I hoped he understood.

# CHAPTER 8

*S*itting in the Principal's office, I felt like I had been a bad
student and was waiting for my punishment. In all my
years, I had never gone to the Principal's office, so it was an experience I never wanted to live again. I didn't even want Jack to experience this. I would make sure he wouldn't.

When Principal Birkman came in, I stood up. I don't know why I
stood up. This was all a nerve wrecking experience for me. I couldn't
see what trouble he could bring when he was such a good boy, especially around me.

"That's all right. Please, sit," Principal Birkman said.

I could feel my nervous energy seeping in even more. He shook
my hand and then told me to take my seat again. I sat down and
waited for him to state why he had called me there the previous week.

"I'm calling about your nephew's behavior problems that he has
been having at the school."

I froze. "Um... yeah, behavior problems? Like what kind?" I asked.

He opened up a folder and withdrew a few papers. He looked them
over and started telling me about a couple of the teachers having
problems with him. He was speaking up in front of the class and he
doesn't seem to have his homework to turn in. That last part confused

me because I knew that he was doing his homework. In a calm state, I explained that.

"I sit at home and help him with his homework, so I know that he's doing it. And things have been rough in his home life. I won't even lie about that."

"Yes, I don't know what's going on, but I heard that you're taking care of him, is that correct?"

I heaved a sigh. "I don't know how temporary or permanent it is," I admitted. "I mean, I have attempted to reach out to my sister, but she hasn't responded to any of my calls." I shrugged. "I really don't know what's going on with her."

He nodded and gave me an apologetic look. "I know that it must be tough for Jack, but we can't have his outbursts in class. It is disruptive, and I wanted to make sure you were aware." He hesitated, before continuing. "Your nephew has never caused any complaints with any of the staff or teachers. So, I know this is most likely an aftermath of his current situation. I hear he joined basketball, is that correct?"

I nodded. "Yes, he loves it."

"Then that's good! I trust that things will improve for him. I don't want to burden you with all this. I know it has to be hard for you too. I also know that you would want to know if there are any issues going on at the school with him."

He was right that I would. The biggest concern I had, was the fact that he wasn't turning in his homework. Every night I would make sure he finished his homework. Was he not telling me that he had more to do? I couldn't see Jack lying to me either. I promised Principal Birkman that I would make sure Jack straightened up. I then shook his hand and left his office.

For the most part, it wasn't as bad as it could have been in there. As I left the school and went to work, I was still thinking a lot about it. I didn't get much done at work until after lunch when I got a call from Braxton Washington's office.

"Hello?" I recognized the number right away.

"Hello. Is this Addison Cole?" The woman on the line asked.

"This is she," I responded.

"I'm calling about the proposal you gave us," she said.

"Yes," I waited with anticipation.

"Well, the executives liked you and they want you as their real estate agent."

I was overcome with eagerness as I thanked her and then hung up. This would definitely be a client that would bring great things to me. It would put me on the map as far as real estate.

The rest of the day I was excited about the call. By the grace of God, I was their real estate agent. I had to find them property quick. With Jack now staying with me and living expenses going up, I needed money to roll in quick. There was now a little more pep in my workload. How could I even date especially with this added work-load? I made the right decision declining Isaac date. There was just too much going on right now in my life.

I finished up early and went to school to pick up Jack. I still needed to have a conversation with him. I needed to make sure that he understood what the Principal said was going on. When he got in the car, I started off to see how his day went.

"How was your day?" I asked, pulling away from the curb.

"Good," he mumbled.

"Was it?" I asked. He looked up and nodded, catching my stare in the rearview mirror. I looked back to the road as I continued. "So, I saw Principal Birkman this morning, and he told me that you haven't been turning in your homework. But you've gotten it done, right? So, I don't understand why."

He looked nervous to talk about it. I figured that the only way to get him to talk, would be to withhold something important from him, so I tried that.

"If you can't tell me what's going on, then we should skip basket-ball practice tonight."

His eyes widened, and he sighed, then looked out the window. "Some kids pick on me," he started. "I want them to like me, so I give them my homework." He looked back and I could see the pain in his eyes. "I also tend to act out in class, because they laugh and I know they like me then."

I felt awful to see him struggling. "What kids?" I asked. I turned into my driveway and when I parked, we sat there talking.

"Just some kids. Aunt Addison, I don't want to get them into trouble. I'll be fine. It's getting better and I promise that I won't do it again. Please, don't ask for their names."

I nodded and told him I wouldn't. "Let's go inside. We have some things to get done before practice. We got out of the car and headed to the front door. It was just one more thing on my list of things I needed to pray about. Jack was being bullied, and I knew that prayer would help in a situation like this.

※

*I* got back to the school, and we parked. I had already decided that I wouldn't stay inside during the practice. I didn't want to find myself looking at Isaac, in the same light that he looked at me. But I went inside with Jack to drop him off and thought I could escape the coach when I ran into him as I was leaving.

"Where are you going?" he asked.

"I have some things to do during practice, so I'll be back to pick him up," I said.

"Oh!" He looked disappointed as he said that.

I smiled and moved past him, but his voice caught me and I turned back around. "Hey... about church yesterday," he started. "I hope you believe me when I say that it was a huge coincidence, but a coincidence nonetheless."

I nodded. "I do believe you."

"Good, because I haven't found a church where I had a connection such as that one and I want to keep going back. I hope that's not a problem for you."

I thought about telling him I would appreciate him going somewhere else, but that wasn't good to say. I shook my head. "That's no problem at all and, besides, I can't exactly tell you what church you can and can't attend, can I?"

He smiled, and I turned back around. I left the gymnasium, but that still small voice was questioning the move I was making at that moment. It was like He didn't want me to leave and wait in the car. In fact, the Holy Spirit was telling me to go back into the gymnasium. I stopped and heeded the prompting of the Holy Spirit even though I didn't want to go back in.

As I sat on the bleachers, I saw Isaac smile when he noticed I had returned. I threw up my hands and sat down watching him. There was something about him that made my mind go to mush and my heart get a little fuller. I took my journal out of my bag and started to write and pray:

*Dear Future Husband,*

*Bullied... I don't know why bullies have to exist, but our own Jack is experiencing that right now. He's such a good boy, and he has so much love inside him. I don't like to know that he is going through some difficult times, upon the separation of his mother. What I would tell the bullies if given a chance, is that they should realize they don't need to do that to get what they want. All they need to do is ask for some help and they will get it. Instead, they seek out those little ones like my Jack.*

*When I had the talk with Principal Birkman, I knew that there had to be more to the story. I didn't fathom that this was it. I know that some might think that Jack would only tell me his part of the story, but he's not that type. Anyone that meets him, will be able to see his heart. And you, dear husband, I know will get a front-row view of it very soon. I can't wait for you to become a part of my life and see the good that is in Jack.*

*He smiles when he plays basketball. I know that might be the one thing he truly finds joy with right now, but I'm opening him up to new things. He went to church, and he said that he loved it. It wasn't even just something where he sort of liked it. He said that he loved it. His excitement impressed me when he had discussed what he learned at Children's Church. So, he will get there and I will help him get there. But soon I hope it will be that we will get him there together. I look forward to that day.*

*Always and Forever,*
*Addison*
*P.S. I am the new realtor of Braxton Washington, the owner of*

*Washington Industries. I am so excited and wish you were here to celebrate with me by taking me out to dinner. Well, no worries. Soon we will celebrate a lot of great things. It's only a matter of time.*

I closed my eyes and began to pray. I didn't care who was around.

*Father,*

*I want to thank you for the opportunities and doors you have opened up for me. This new deal with Mr. Washington is so wonderful. You've seen me work hard and you've been there each step of the way guiding me and leading me to this place. I am forever grateful.*

*Looking at this opportunity helps me to see so many things. If Mr. Washington can search for me, my future husband will do the same because of you leading the way. I know for sure that if you could do that, you will definitely send the man you have for me very soon. I have to remain faithful, committed, and obedient to you.*

*Lord, I also take this time to pray for Jack. Help me with dealing with this situation. I pray that any bullies that are bothering and hindering Jack stop or remove them right now. I pray that you will also help Jack to have the strength to stand up to his bullies. Give him the words to say. Give him the mindset and the plan to deal with these bullies. Let it all work out for his good.*

*Father, help Jack to be the best in his class. Help him not to act out. Help him to be respectful to his peers and to teachers. I pray that things will improve in his life. I thank You, Father.*

*In Jesus' Name, Amen!*

# CHAPTER 9

*A* little more than a week went by and things with Jack and I only seemed to improve. He would open up to me in ways that he never did before and we became closer in the process. I was happy to see that the week also brought no more calls from the Principal. According to Jack, things at school were even better.

He also improved in basketball. Having the extra practices with Isaac seemed to help. Things between Isaac and myself always seemed to be on a different path than what he had in mind earlier. As he didn't approach me about going out again. He did go to church that following Sunday. Somehow, wound up sitting in the same aisle, but he was a safe enough distance away.

There was something about Isaac that I couldn't shake. I had to keep reminding myself that it was about Jack and work. Those were the only things that I couldn't give my full attention to. Although, it seemed as the days went on I was thinking more and more about him. Some days I would have to catch myself because I started to daydream about him and us. Thoughts ran through my brain. Thoughts of how good-looking and talented he was. He also had a way with kids and the way he cared for Jack melted my heart. Something was invading my heart as I thought about him. What was this feeling I was feeling?

Peace filled my heart and somehow he was pulling me in even though I was trying my best to fight it.

*"Isn't this what you want and what you have been praying for?" I asked myself as I clicked away on the computer mouse.*

So many reasons filled my mind about why I couldn't be with Isaac. It wasn't a good time. I had work. I have new clients. I have Jack now. As much as I wanted love, how could I fit it into my schedule? I stopped clicking whatever was on the screen and sat back in my chair. As I pressed my fingertips together another question came to my mind. *Why was I pushing this away?*

I had been writing in my journal and I had been praying for my future husband. I even asked God to send him very soon. Could this be the answer to my prayers finally? I bowed my head to pray because I was becoming overwhelmed with so many thoughts. Whenever thoughts like that flooded my mind, I've learned to pray and seek God.

"Okay, God, please speak to my heart," I said, now closing my eyes.

As soon as I asked God to speak to my heart, a loud sound came from my computer notifying me that an email had come through. My coworker from across the hall always sent me stories from time to time. The title, The Drowning Man, intrigued me. I decided to click and read it:

A religious man was in floodwaters that were rising. He went to the roof of his house and trusted that God would rescue him. One of his neighbors came by in a small boat and said, "The waters will be above your house very soon. Why don't you hop in and we will get to safety together?"

"No," said the religious man. "I've already prayed and God will save me."

Later someone else came by in a bigger boat and said the same thing as the first man. The man replied again, "I've already prayed and God will save me."

Not long after that a rescue helicopter hovered above him and let down a ladder. Again, he was told that the waters will be above his house and that he should climb up the ladder and fly to safety.

Again, he says, "No, I've already prayed and God will save me."

During this time the floodwaters rose, and it reached above the roof and the man drowned. He got to heaven and when he saw God he asked, "Why am I here in heaven? You said you would save me. I trusted you. I prayed."

God shook his head and said, "Yes, I did save you. I sent boats and a helicopter but you never got in."

I let out a laugh. God always came through when I needed Him to. I was praying and asking God to give me the desires of my heart daily. Here I was turning what could be the answers to my prayers down. The words, you never got in, stuck to me like hot glue.

"All right God, I get it," I said out loud.

I closed the email smiling, but I almost fell out of my chair when I saw the time. With all this thinking, reading stories, and looking at land for Mr. Washington, I didn't notice time was escaping me. We had a practice planned for after school that day with Isaac. By the time I caught a glimpse of the clock, the practice would be over before I got there.

I folded up important papers and placed them into an empty envelope. I dialed up Isaac's number on my cell phone. It rang three times before he picked up. "Hello?"

"Hey, it's Addison. I'm sorry, but I'm running behind. Will you please stay with him until I get there?"

"Of course," he said. "See you in a few."

He disconnected the call. I ran out of the office, jumped in my car and tore out of there. I hated being a burden on anyone, especially someone like Isaac. He probably had more important things to do than wait with Jack. I pulled into the parking lot and grabbed a spot right at the door. I then jumped out with my purse and hurried up the walkway. When I got in the gymnasium, I slowed my pace a bit.

Jack and Isaac were shooting baskets together, and it was a nice picture to have in mind. I stopped walking and watched them as they enjoyed their time with one another. He was the perfect guy if I was looking for someone that would be a good role model for Jack. I couldn't ask for a better fit. After gawking at them for several minutes, I made my presence known by speaking up.

"Hey, buddy! Ready to go?"

Jack dropped the ball and turned around. He looked upset to have to leave but then nodded. "Thanks, Coach Isaac," he said. He looked up at Isaac. Coach Isaac smiled and nodded.

"My pleasure, little man." He tossed me a look. "I'll walk you out." I opened my mouth to argue, but before I could, he was falling into step with me. We were leaving the gymnasium together. We walked over to my car and Jack went around and got in the backseat. I turned around to look at the man that was two inches from me.

"I appreciate you helping me out. I'm sorry that I overlooked the time."

He shrugged my worries away. "Don't even think about it. I was glad to help. He's a special guy."

I smiled and nodded. "He is. Thank you!" I grabbed the door handle and hesitated as I looked his way. "Guess I'll see you tomorrow then?"

He nodded, but then interjected. "I know that I've tried asking you this before, but I'm going to ask you again. Won't you please just go out with me to get a cup of coffee or something? There doesn't have to be any strings attached. A nice cup of coffee is all I'm proposing. What do you say?"

I smiled and thought about it, but only for a minute. "I guess that a cup of coffee wouldn't hurt."

He beamed from ear to ear. "Great! We can discuss it more tomorrow."

"Okay then! See you tomorrow."

I got in the driver's seat and he closed the door behind me. I looked out the window, and he waved goodbye to us and then turned around and headed back into the gymnasium. I couldn't believe I had finally accepted that cup of coffee. We both knew it was a date, but the more I thought about it, the more grateful I was that I did accept it.

I pulled out of the parking spot and was turning away from the school when I heard Jack's voice. "I like Coach Isaac," he said. "He's nice!"

I smiled and knew then that I had made the right choice. "I agree. I like him too," I said. I didn't have to divulge more information than that.

We got home and went straight inside. Jack went up and started his routine. It was bath first and then get ready for bed while I would start to make the supper. However, tonight, I changed things up a bit by first going for my journal. I wanted to get my letter written before I would forget some things I wanted to say. I grabbed it and sat down in the chair, then started off my letter:

*Dear Future Husband*

*Something happened tonight that makes me wonder if I might have found you. I said yes to Isaac's invitation to go out. So, more than a couple weeks have gone by since he first asked and now I feel confident in saying yes. I am so grateful that God has given me so much strength. But now I have to wonder what I'll wear, what will I say, what will I do if he attempts to kiss me. There are so many what-ifs. Right now I'm trying to focus on the amazing feeling that I have of someone wanting to go out with me.*

*And... it makes it all that much better that Jack seems to like him. So, I know that I should put my own insecurities and feelings of having too much on my plate behind me and do this. If for no other reason than the fact that Jack likes him. Yet, it's not that I don't like him. In fact, I am finding that I am attracted to him and he makes me smile and laugh, but he's just an all-around good person. So, I could very much see him fit this bill. The one that I've been searching for. I am desperate to find you and still holding onto all hope.*

*Forever and Always,*

*Addison*

# CHAPTER 10

*I* couldn't wait for Saturday afternoon to come. That was the day that we had set up to go out for coffee and it all conveniently worked out. Jack had a friend's house he could go to, while I was with Isaac. We both agreed that it would be best not to tell Jack that we were going out. I didn't want Jack to get too excited. If things didn't work out, I didn't want to upset him and cause a bad relationship between them on the basketball court.

"I'll be back to pick you up in a couple hours," I said, as I left him off at Troy's house.

"Okay. Bye Aunt Addison," he called out as he headed up to the front door. I watched him as he rang the bell, then waited for someone to answer. Troy's mother was at the door. We waved to each other, and I then pulled away heading off to the coffee shop. This was going to be simple enough. It would be coffee and that was it, I kept telling myself.

When I pulled into the coffee shop, I noticed that there were only a few cars in the parking lot. Isaac was getting out of his vehicle as I arrived. I looked at myself in the rearview mirror and took a deep breath as I tried to calm my nerves. I got out of the car and headed to the front door where Isaac still was.

He glanced at me and grinned his greeting. "Hello, Addison."

"Hello!"

He looked me over. "You look nice."

I blushed. He had every word to say in the right manner. "Thanks!" I swallowed the lump in my throat.

"And these are for you," he said handing me some pink roses.

I blushed. No one had ever given me roses on a first date. On top of that, pink was my favorite color.

"Thank you!" I smiled while taking them. "These are beautiful."

He then opened the door for me and I stepped inside. "Thank you!" He was a gentleman, but I had no doubt he would be.

We went up to the counter and ordered two coffees. I reached for my money, but he stopped me.

"I got it," I argued, but there was no getting through to him, so I accepted it. I didn't want to start off things with an argument.

We went to a table and sat down and the conversation seemed to flow so smoothly. I was nervous and anxious about what the date would bring, but it seemed like there was no reason for my nervousness. Isaac was a nice guy that no matter what, I knew we would be great friends.

"How are things going with you?" he asked. "I mean, in relation to the sudden guardianship of your nephew."

"Well, I'm trying to get by. It is rough because I wasn't used to being a mother and so it was all new territory, but every day it's getting easier. It's what families do."

He took a drink of his coffee, then looked a little worried about asking the next question. "Do you want to talk about what happened?" he asked.

Since Brianna left Jack in my care, I never opened up to anyone. Coming on the date, I didn't expect opening up to him either. Yet, fifteen minutes in and I'm already talking about it. "I got a call and Brianna was upset. She said that she couldn't handle raising him alone anymore and that she needed me to take him. There was no getting through to her, no matter how hard I tried." I could remember that conversation like it was yesterday. "I've tried reaching out to her, but since getting that phone call, she won't answer any of my calls. You know, that's the hardest thing that's come from all this. I'm losing my sister and Jack's losing his mother."

"Wow! I can't even imagine," he said. He stopped drinking his coffee to take in everything that I said and it brought us even closer. It was good having someone to talk to. It was good having someone other than my journal that would listen.

"Tell me about your family," I stated. "Any siblings?"

"Nope. I'm an only child."

I scrunched up my nose. "You're one of those individuals." That got us laughing. We went on to discussing everything else that we wanted to know in the span of a couple of hours. Before I knew it, three hours had passed, and the waitress filled our cups once more.

"Want any pie?" she asked us.

"Do you?" he inquired. "I'm thinking a nice apple pie would hit the spot."

He reached for his wallet, but I glanced at the time and figured that it was better yet that we decided to end this. We could resume it for another day, or at least I hoped we would. "Sounds great, but I should be going to pick up Jack," I said.

He nodded and put his wallet away. "Thanks anyway," he said.

The waitress left, and I took a quick drink from my coffee mug and then we stood up. He followed close behind me as we went outside and wound up standing at my car. "I did have a nice time today, Isaac."

He smiled. "So did I. I'm hoping we can do it again."

I nodded. There wasn't any doubt that I wanted to. "I would like that." I opened the door and got in the front seat. "Hope you enjoy the rest of your day."

"You too!" He waved to me as he shut the door and I started my car. The date couldn't have gone any better, and I was already anticipating the moment where we would do it again.

❄

*I* picked up Jack at his friend's house and I almost didn't want to break him up from that. They looked like they were having a blast, but I eventually had to and we headed back home. When we got there and were inside, I started up.

"Hey, bud, run upstairs and clean your room. I saw it before heading out and it is atrocious and doesn't look like you've cleaned it since you've gotten here." I laughed, not thinking it would be that big of a deal. As I was looking through the cupboards in the kitchen for what I would make for supper, I heard sounds from the television. I could tell the TV was on.

I left the kitchen and went to the living room where Jack was watching a show. "What are you doing?" I asked.

"Watching TV," he answered, not even looking up. I walked over to the television and shut it off, then turned around to face him. He gave me a frustrated look.

"I told you to clean your room."

He shrugged. "I will after I get done," he said with an attitude.

"No! You'll do it now and then you can watch TV," I stated.

He stood up and put his hands on his waist and glared at me. "You're not my mom and you can't tell me what to do." He stood up from the couch, the look on his face spoke volumes and I had a sting in my chest as he said those words.

"I never said I was your mom, but this is my house and I told you to go clean your room. You'll be abiding by my rules. Go upstairs and do as I've said," I ordered.

"Mom wouldn't make me do that. She would say I deserve a rest. I don't want to." He was throwing a tantrum, and it was a side of him that I wasn't privy to seeing.

"I'm sorry that your mother didn't make you do it, but that's one of the ways that we'll differ. Don't get me started on your mother's bad habits."

His eyes got big, and I knew I struck a nerve because I could tell that tears weren't far behind. "I hate you!" He yelled. He turned around and ran up the stairs and I heard him slam the bedroom door. I stood there for a moment, feeling my own tears ready to spill over.

I didn't know how I thought I could manage to date right now when there was so much still going on in Jack's life. He had to be my priority. I took a deep breath and wiped away the few tears at the corner of my eyes. Then, I grabbed my cell phone from my pocket and dialed up Isaac's number. I didn't want to lose the nerve, and this was something I needed to do.

"Hello? I was just thinking about you." He laughed on the other end and it tore at my insides.

"Hey! So, I need to be honest with you and myself. This isn't going to work out," I said.

"What? I don't understand. I thought you had a good time?"

"And I did. You have no idea how nice it was, but Jack needs me and I can't focus on anything but that. I hope you understand."

"I understand that precedence has to be with your nephew, but is there anything I can do?" he asked. It was nice that he offered, but this was something that only I could handle.

"There isn't, but I'll let you know if I think of anything," I said.

"All right then! If you change your mind, you know where to find me." His voice sounded like someone that had been dumped and it was only one date.

"I know. I'll see you later!" I quickly hung up, for fear I would start crying on the other end. I then went up the stairs and stood outside of Jack's room to listen to see if any movement was heard inside. I heard some sniffling, and it broke my heart, but he needed space.

I went to my own room and stood there for a moment. I closed the door behind me and went to my bed where I knelt down at the foot of it.

"God, I don't know why you would bring this man into my life now, when I can't work on a relationship. I wanted things to be good for us. I wanted to date Isaac, but the timing is terrible. So God... why... why now?"

I looked up at the ceiling and tears started to stream down my cheeks. I closed my eyes and relaxed.

"Why God? It's an impossible situation to get into. You have left me single for so long, then You bring Jack into my life. I can't focus on a relationship when Jack is acting like this. Just when I think I've found someone, I have to break it off before it even begins because of this new responsibility. I'm angry God, so give me answers."

I remained in that state for several minutes until the tears died down and I could get back up. I needed to get supper ready and try to salvage my relationship with Jack before it was too late.

❄

*J*ack came downstairs and ate, but that was about all I could say. He didn't want to talk to me. He didn't even respond when I asked him a question. So, we ate in peace and when we were through, he mumbled that he was going back upstairs and I cleaned the dishes.

After cleaning the kitchen, I went into the living room. I grabbed the journal, then sat down on the chair and opened it up to the next empty page. I wrote out my letter even though I really wasn't feeling it at the moment:

*Dear Future Husband,*

*Today has been a whirlwind of emotions. At one moment, I'm stoked about going out with this amazing guy. He's a guy that I know could be you, and then the next minute I'm yelling at Jack because of him not wanting to follow my rules. I know that things with him can only improve with time, but just when I think I'm getting through to him, this happens. It's another setback.*

*I knew that I needed to end things with Isaac right away. How can I work on finding a man to love me when I have such turmoil going on in my life right now? It's been so long since I've gotten down on my knees and bawled out for God to listen to me, but that's exactly what I did. I have been seeking you out for years and when I think I found you, you're pulled out of my grasp. I don't think it is fair, but I have never been the one to say 'why me?'*

*And I don't feel I should say that now. I want answers. I want everything to all workout and I don't think I'm asking for all that much.*

*I know you would have wise words if you were here. You would comfort me and tell me that Jack is going to be fine. You would tell me that I'm going to be fine and that we've been through so much together. In the end, he will see that I am only trying to help him out. I am proud of the kid he is and I believe that despite what he's going through, he will grow from this. I want him to allow me the chance to be here for him, without pushing me away. Maybe once that happens, then I can go back to seeking out God's will for my love life and that will one day bring me back to you.*

*Always and Forever,*

*Addison*

I was looking at the journal when I heard shuffling on the stairs and then his voice. "Aunt Addison?" I looked up.

"Yes?" I asked.

"I'm sorry. I don't hate you." He looked so sad and I sighed and stood up from where I was sitting. I walked over to him and knelt down in front of him, then pulled him into a hug.

"I know you don't, buddy." We stayed in that position and I felt like crying once more, but this time happier tears, because I wasn't losing Jack. We still needed to find our balance, but there was plenty of time for that.

# CHAPTER 11

*A* few weeks went by and I did everything in my power to steer clear of Isaac. I had to admit that I thought I did a pretty good job with that. I sent Jack in to practice on his own and we started going to the first-morning church service. However, a few times, Jack would come out to the car from practice, only to say, "Coach Isaac asked about you today. Why don't you come to my practices?" He asked. "You should see me. I'm doing much better."

"That's good to hear," I would say ignoring his main question.

I knew that I wouldn't be able to do that forever, especially when he had a couple games coming up. I felt that I had to be there, plus I wanted to be there. So, I needed to put my thoughts aside and just do it, even if I was uncomfortable with the situation.

The one thing that I couldn't be happier for though, was the fact that Jack, and I were getting closer with our bond. As the days went on, he even stopped asking when his mom was coming back. We had gone back to the old house to get the things he wanted to bring with him, especially all his clothes. We even tried to put it out of our mind that Brianna was ever coming back.

There wasn't a day that went by, though, that I didn't think about her. Sometimes, I'd find myself calling her phone, on the off chance that she would one day pick up. Of course, that didn't happen. It was disappointing. I could no longer question my sister's motives when things between Jack were getting better. I even received a call from Principal Birkman telling me that he wasn't sure what I said to him, but it was working. Jack was no longer giving his teachers problems, and he was even on the road to the Honor Roll. That made me a proud aunt, but all credit goes to God because it was His doing.

Now, on Friday night, a month after I stopped things with Isaac, I had to swallow my pride. I had to go to the basketball game to root on Jack. I knew I would definitely have to see him, but hoped to escape the gymnasium without talking to him.

Jack was right though, he had gotten better, and it impressed me when he made three baskets. He even got a three-pointer. All that practice time with Isaac had paid off for him and I couldn't be rooting for him any more than I already was.

The home team ended up winning by a few baskets, but it was a win, nonetheless. We all jumped up and cheered. It was exciting. Several parents even went running down the bleachers to congratulate their child. I did the same. I met up with Jack and he was grinning from ear to ear.

"Congratulations!" I said. I hugged him tightly. "I'm so proud of you."

"Thanks, Aunt Addison," he said. When we parted, he started talking with so much excitement. "Did you see that three-pointer?" he asked.

I laughed. "I sure did. You did an awesome job. Go get changed and I'll take you out for pizza," I said.

He ran off, and I watched him disappear in the locker room.

"He did well, didn't he?"

I turned around to find Isaac heading towards me. I nodded. "His coach knows his stuff." I was flirting with him. It came naturally and seeing him there made me remember how much I liked this guy. He brought me pink roses on the first date for goodness' sake. Most guys don't do that nowadays. Why God? I asked myself.

"A coach can't teach someone if they don't want to learn," he responded. He then hesitated before asking. "Hey, a group of the guys asked me to go with them to get something to eat to celebrate the victory. Do you guys want to come?"

I spotted Jack hurrying out towards us and I shook my head. "I'm sorry, but we should be getting home. It's late. You guys have a good time."

He frowned but nodded. "Thanks!" He then exchanged some generous words with Jack and then Jack and I headed out of the gym and to my car. In my mind, I wanted to go with them. I was certain that Jack would want to too, but I knew that I had made the right choice. I shivered as we got in the car. It was the middle of November and the weather was proving that it was going to be a cold winter.

"Buckle up, Bud," I said as I started the car. I pulled out of the parking lot. Jack started jabbering away about how awesome the game was and how he hoped all his games were like that. I smiled and listened to him go on and on about the game. I thought that if every day he was as happy as he was right then, then I wouldn't have any issues and maybe I could date again.

We went to the pizzeria, but it worried me that we would run into Isaac and the rest of the team, so we took the pizza to go. Jack didn't even question it. When we got home and was eating pizza in the living room, in front of the fireplace, Jack posed the question. "Aunt Addison?" he asked.

"What is it?" I asked, taking a bite of the slice of pizza.

"Will Coach Isaac ever come over? He's a nice guy and I think sometimes he might be lonely."

I smiled as I thought about that. That was a perception I didn't expect someone of Jack's age to have. There was only one way to answer that question, and that was the truth. "I like how you're concerned about people, but Coach Isaac won't be coming to our house."

"Why?" He asked frowning. I didn't know what to say to that question.

"Finish eating your pizza. We'll discuss that later," I said. As he ate,

I pondered over that. It would be way too complicated to explain to a seven-year-old.

When we were both done eating, we put the rest of the pizza in the refrigerator and tossed the paper plates away. He then looked at me. "I'm going to go clean up my room," he said.

I snickered. Things had definitely changed in our household. "Okay!" I watched him leave the kitchen and then went in the living room and grabbed the journal. I sat back down in front of the fireplace and looked through past journal entries. Over the past month, my entries had become longer and more in depth about what I was looking for and what I needed. I knew that was because of how I was missing Isaac and I was gearing all my prayers and entries to him. I flipped back to the next blank page and sat there for a moment, getting lost in the glow of the fire. Then looked down and started to write:

*Dear Future Husband,*

*Every time I look at you, I am reminded of what I want. Every quality that Isaac possesses is what I long for in you. Tonight at the basketball game I saw you and it was like my heart stopped or at least skipped a beat. Your smile has a way of making me believe that everything will be all right.*

*We won the game to boot. Jack was so happy to be out there, you could see it written all over his face. You taught him to be the best player he possibly could be, and he has been. And it breaks my heart to tell him that you can't come over when I want you to come over. I want you to be a part of my life. I don't know why God brought you into my life now. I have pushed you away, dear future husband, because I know that it's the best thing for you and for Jack. I'm not stable right now. Being a guardian of a seven-year-old is a lot right now. I have a ready-made family and I fear that you wouldn't commit to it. Or, at least, that's all that I'm telling myself.*

*So, I make this vow that I'm better off staying single and this is going to help the both of us in the long run. It's a myth and I know that, but I can't get my heart to give in. I want my forever and always, but I'm left once again empty-handed. Will it be too late once I'm ready? I sure hope not.*

*Forever and Always,*

*Addison*

I looked at the journal entry and then closed it. I leaned back against the couch and watched the fire as I prayed.

*Father,*

*I've been single and by myself for such a long time and now I have Jack. He's my concern right now. I'm afraid that dating would take away everything that I am trying to build with him. I don't know how to date and take care of him. When do I even find the time?*

*So I ask you now Father to take away this fear and help me to balance it all. I have a fear that I can't do both. For scripture says, 'For you have not given us a spirit of fear, but of power and love and of a sound mind.' Give me that spirit of love. Yes, help me to love and to balance love.*

*This I pray, in Jesus' Name, Amen!*

As I said amen, I then heard the pitter patter of socks on the stairs. I looked up to see Jack coming around the corner. "Come here," I said.

He walked over and I pulled him onto the couch and hugged him close to me as we both stared at the flames.

"You know I love you, right?" I whispered.

He looked up at me and nodded. "I love you too!" I kissed his forehead and then went back to gazing at the fireplace. He was the only man I needed in my life right now because he made me happy. But there was still a void in my heart and I couldn't help but hope that one day that void would be filled. I didn't want to be like the drowning man so I had to figure this thing out quickly.

# CHAPTER 12

*H*olidays always have a way of approaching at such a fast speed. I couldn't believe that Thanksgiving was just a few days away and this would be the first Thanksgiving without Brianna there. It wasn't going to be the same, but I vowed that I needed Jack to feel like things were going right in his life, so I had to do my best to make it amazing for him. Which meant that I needed to get all the Thanksgiving preparations underway so that we would be ready for a great celebration.

Work was busier than normal for me, but I made sure to not let work drown me because holidays are the time when you're supposed to spend it with family and friends. Jack was my only family left. Mom was gone and now Brianna was nowhere to be found. So, I was grateful that a neighbor of ours from two houses down invited Jack and I over for Thanksgiving but I declined because it needed to be a time we spent at home together, just rejoicing in the things that we were thankful for.

It was the Wednesday night before Thanksgiving and Jack and I was out buying last-minute things for our small dinner. At the supermarket, I rounded the curb with my cart and I literally ran smack dab right into Isaac. I could feel the heat burning my cheeks.

"Coach Isaac!" Jack squealed. He ran up to him and gave him a high-five and even a hug. Despite us seeing him frequently, it was always nice to see Jack's response. Jack has really taken to Isaac.

"Hey, you two! Out getting last minute Turkey Day necessities?" he asked. He shot me a look and smiled and I nodded.

"I'm just here getting a few things. Obviously, we have the turkey already, but what's turkey without cranberry sauce."

He nodded and chuckled lightly. "That is true." He hesitated, glancing at our cart and the looking up at me. "Well, I better leave you guys to it then. Enjoy your Thanksgiving."

We had spent a vast majority of our time ignoring one another. Really, it was me trying to ignore him because I knew that if I didn't I would once again want something to happen, but there was just way too much going on in my life for anything to happen. Isaac was probably still upset with me, so it was no wonder he wanted to cut out of there as quickly as possible. It was Jack that didn't let that happen.

"What are you doing for Thanksgiving? Are you having it with your family?" Jack asked.

Isaac looked at him and he smiled slightly, but something in his eyes said there wasn't much to smile about. "I'm afraid not. My family isn't around here, so I'll probably just go out and get a bite to eat. Or put in a TV dinner." He laughed as if to show us it was a joke, but I could tell he wasn't joking. "I'm sure you guys have a lot to do. If I don't see you before then, you both have a wonderful Thanksgiving. Take care!" He nodded at me and shot a smile to Jack and then turned with his cart and headed in the opposite direction.

It didn't take long for Jack to express his irritation with me, but I also was irritated with myself. That wasn't how a Christian should handle themselves. The minute he said that he had nowhere to be, I should have offered him a place to go and Jack was quick to tell me that.

"Aunt Addison... he has nowhere to go. Can we invite him to our place?" When he called the home our place, I was pleased, because for the first time I felt like maybe he really thought of it as his home. I sighed, knowing that Jack was right.

"Wait right here!" I kept him at the cart as I hurried after him. When I rounded the corner, I found him looking at the frozen dinners. He looked so sad. My heart melted and I put my differences aside and mustered up the courage to speak with him again.

"Hey..." He turned, looking startled to find me there.

"Hey, Addison. What's up?" He tossed the dinner into his cart and turned to me. I fidgeted on my legs as I stepped from one foot to the other, unsure how to ask him. So, I just did it.

"If you really aren't doing anything on Thursday, we would love for you to join us at our place. It's not overly exciting, and it's just going be us, but you're welcome to join us."

He smiled. "That's a sweet offer, but I can't put you out," he argued.

I shook my head. "It's not putting us out. I would be happy to have you there."

He smiled. "Okay then! Text me the address and time and I'll be there."

"I will." I turned on my heel and headed back to the cart where Jack gave me an expectant look. "He'll be there," I said.

He clapped his hands with glee. "I'm excited."

I then frowned. "You didn't want to have it with just me?" I asked.

He laughed. "Coach Isaac didn't have anywhere to go, so this is the right thing to do."

He was such a grown man for his age. I pushed his head with my hand, and he chuckled as we moved on to the rest of the grocery list. Jack was right. In my heart, I knew this was the only decision I could make with a clear heart, but suddenly I was nervous about Thursday and hoped it wasn't a complete disaster.

❄

The smell of a Thanksgiving meal would always get anyone excited, but I was nervous that something would happen to make everything fall apart. And when the doorbell rang at ten minutes until noon worry heightened in intensity. "Will you get the door?" I asked Jack.

He ran off to get the door, and I took off my apron and tried to look presentable, then laughed at myself because it wasn't like I was intending on impressing anyone. I just didn't want to look a mess. I turned around when I heard his voice.

"It smells amazing in here."

I blushed and thanked him and then noticed the flowers in his hands and the apple pie in the other. I moved closer to him. "Thank you! The food will be done any second."

"These are for you," he said. He handed over red roses. I grinned and thanked him, then took them and went over and put them in a vase with some water. He followed me with the apple pie in hand.

"Look what he gave me!" I looked to the side and saw Jack holding a new basketball. I glanced at Isaac.

"You didn't need to do that," I said.

He shrugged. "Didn't want to come empty-handed. Maybe we can shoot some hoops later," he said.

"That will be awesome!" Jack said. He left the kitchen, leaving Isaac and I awkwardly standing around, but I was pleasantly surprised to see it wasn't all that awkward.

"You've made his day if not his month," I said, laughing.

He grinned. "I'm glad I could." He then looked around the small kitchen.

"Oh, let me take that. Did you make it?" I asked wondering if he could cook.

"I sure did! My mother's famous apple pie."

"Really?" I asked surprised.

"Yes, indeed. I don't make this special pie or give red roses to just anyone. This pie is special and only a special woman deserves to taste its incredibleness," he said laughing.

I took the pie thinking there he goes again. Placing the pie on the table I couldn't help but smile at his comment. He was a persistent one.

"Anything I can do to help?" he asked.

I was impressed that he would make such an offer, but I was nearly finished and there wasn't any reason to get more hands in the kitchen. "I think I'm good, but thanks."

"My pleasure."

I went back to check on the turkey and stuffing and at noon sharp we were ready to serve dinner. At that point I allowed him to help me take the things out and put a buffet of food for the taking. I even allowed Isaac to carve the turkey. He carved it with such pride and joy. He was so happy to do it. Then the three of us loaded up plates, and we were ready to sit down and eat.

After we had all sat down, it was Isaac that asked if he could say the prayer. I nodded, and we joined hands and he began.

"Heavenly Father, I want to thank you for this blessed day when family and friends come together and celebrate everything they are thankful for. It is for you dear God that we are most thankful and as we enjoy fellowship and great conversation through this wonderful meal that Addison prepared, remind us of all the blessings we truly have in life. For those are worth celebrating. We ask you this in Jesus' name. Amen!"

"Amen!" I whispered. "Thank you!" I said.

We each sat there, not eating, and I felt like bringing another tradition back. "Growing up, my family didn't have a lot, but every Thanksgiving we wanted to celebrate in what we did have, no matter how little it might seem and after we recite a scripture verse. So, I was hoping that today we could continue that tradition. We each get to express what we are most thankful for in the past year and we say a scripture verse."

Isaac was very accepting of that and I offered for him to go first. "There is truly so much I'm thankful for," he said. "For starters, I am thankful that you were generous enough to open up your home to me today. It was very nice of you and I appreciate it."

I smiled as he continued.

"When I got the job at the school, working as the coach, I left my family and friends to start a new chapter in my life. I never expected to meet such wonderful people, but I have. I am thankful for those that I have met over the past couple months. I am thankful for finding a church that I absolutely love. And I'm thankful that I'm healthy and my friends are healthy." He grinned. "Oh and I'm thankful for all those young and talented basketball players that I get to coach this year and that will make the NBA someday." He turned to Jack, who was beaming like he had just won a brand new bike. "Lastly, my scripture verse is one I thought of when I was going to buy a TV Dinner. I had just thought it and was praying in my heart and the scripture is from Genesis 2:18 which says, 'And the LORD God said, It is not good that the man should be alone; I will make him a help meet for him.' Then, you came around the corner to invite me here."

Jack looked right into Isaac's face and chuckled. I too looked at Jack, shook my head and joined in the laughter. Then, Isaac turned to me and I looked over at Jack.

"What are you thankful for Jack?" I asked.

He scrunched up his nose in serious thought before starting. "I am thankful for Coach Isaac as he has taught me to be a better shooter. I do hope to be in the NBA one day." Isaac was smiling at him and his eyes were shining with an appreciation for Jack. "I'm thankful that I have a warm place to come home to."

When he said that my heart broke a little, and I turned to him, but he wasn't finished.

"I'm thankful for Aunt Addison for wanting me when my mom left me and didn't want me anymore."

That last statement broke my heart. I reached out and touched his hand and he looked at me. There were tears in my eyes that I had to get rid of because I shouldn't be crying at a time like this.

"I'm thankful for all of my toys and the video games that Aunt Addison always tells me to turn off and go to bed when I just want to sit there and play. Hopefully, next year I can say I am thankful that she lets me play until I am tired of playing it."

We laughed. He was such a jokester at times. I quickly wiped a tear from my eye before he finished.

"I'm thankful for beating the Uncharted games too."

I smiled. The last two comments were more of a speech and

weren't something so serious but I enjoyed it nonetheless. He shrugged. "That's all!"

"We will have to talk about that Uncharted game. It's a good game but all that cursing for a young boy like yourself, you don't need to be playing that."

"Aunt Addison," he wined.

"She's right buddy," Isaac chimed in. "We will have to find some good Christian video games for you."

"Well, I'm so grateful that Aunt Addison lets me play games like that. They are so fun and I learn so much history from it," he said winking his eye with that sweet boyish face that was getting to my soft side. He always knew how to do it too.

"What's your scripture, buddy?" I asked.

"My scripture is 1 Corinthians 13:7. Love never gives up, never loses faith, is always hopeful, and endures through every circumstance."

I couldn't believe my ears. I expected a simple scripture like Jesus wept, but he came out the woodworks with that one.

"Where did you learn that?" I asked.

"I learned it Sunday School. Our teacher has been talking about love. She made us each memorize a scripture from 1 Corinthians 13:4-7. I was given that one."

I could feel Isaac's eyes now on me. I looked directly into his and in my head, four words rung clear: endures through every circumstance. Would Isaac really want to endure through every circumstance which includes Jack?

# CHAPTER 13

*I* slowly pulled my hand away from Jack. It was touched by his speech and scripture. I pulled my eyes from Isaac as well when Jack asked me what I was thankful for.

"I'm thankful for Jack of course because he has shown me true love and that can't be taken for granted. I'm thankful for my sister who entrusted me with the most important thing to her."

Even if Brianna didn't see it, it was true. Jack was the greatest gift to her, and she returned him like a worn out shirt she didn't wear anymore.

"I'm thankful that we can gather today and I didn't burn the turkey." Isaac snickered and our eyes met again. "I'm thankful for friends that have been there for Jack and helped him along the way. I'm thankful to God, for giving us this life. I'm thankful for every time Jack yells... where are my shoes?" Jack laughed, and I looked around the table at the food. "I'm thankful for a job that can provide this food for us. I'm also thankful for getting an account with Mr. Washington," I smiled and clapped my hands in joy. "Since we are on love scriptures, I might as well add to it. 1 Corinthians 13:13 says, 'And now these three remain: faith, hope, and love. But the greatest of these is love.' And before our stomachs start growling, let's eat."

The three of us laughed and started to eat our food when Isaac spoke up. "I mean it, Addison. This was great that you invited me. Thank you so much!"

"Not a problem," I said. "After all, Jack did kind of beg me to invite you." I laughed and Isaac joined in.

"So, the truth comes out. I should have known. So, thank you, Jack." That got us both to chuckle and I silently went back to eating my food.

"So, what are your Thanksgiving traditions typically?" I asked him. "I mean if you were back with your family, what would you be doing?"

"Well, it would be much like this. The difference being that there would be about forty other people milling around. I come from a pretty big family. We would eat at maybe three and then play games later. We always stayed until at least midnight or after. It's a pretty big deal at home."

"Would everyone go to your parents?" she asked.

"Usually my aunt's and uncle's house," he replied.

We then ate for several minutes, keeping the silence going, until Jack started talking about basketball and the conversation got drowned out. I didn't mind. It was nice just relaxing at the table and not be expected to hold on a lengthy conversation.

When we were done eating, we cleared the table, and he offered to help me with the dishes. I smiled. "No, you relax. It's not necessary. They can wait. If you want to go play basketball with Jack that is fine with me."

"All righty then! The meal was amazing, even better than it smelled. Thanks!"

I nodded. "You're welcome!" I watched him leave the kitchen and Jack and he grabbed a coat, then headed outside to play basketball. When the door closed, I reached into my pocket and withdrew my phone. I knew it was probably no use, but I dialed up Brianna's number. It went straight to voicemail. I decided to leave a message.

"Hey, sis. It's me. So, Happy Thanksgiving to you. I hope you have a nice one. I miss you. Jack misses you too. Just please call. I love you and this is tearing me up inside. Please..."

I quickly hung up before I started to cry and she heard me. I walked over to the front window where they were shooting baskets in the hoop that came with the house. Jack was having a wonderful time, and I didn't want anything to mess that up. I just had to put on a happy face and pretend that everything was all right. It was what was best for Jack.

※

ack and Isaac stayed outside for two hours playing basketball and when they came in, they both looked chilled.

"Brrrrr... it feels more like December out there, than November," Isaac said.

"I'll make some hot chocolate," I said.

"That sounds yummy," Jack said warming his hands up. "Can we watch a Christmas movie? You want to Coach Isaac?"

I smiled and glanced at Isaac. He looked a little bombarded. "Maybe he has other plans," I said. "I mean, he might not want to stay two hours," I said.

Jack looked disappointed.

"I don't want to wear out my welcome," Isaac said.

I looked at him. "You aren't. If you want to stay, then you're welcome."

He nodded. "Then I'll stay!"

"Okay!" Jack pulled Isaac into the other room and I went on to make the hot chocolate. When I was finished with three mugs, I carried them back into the living room and found Jack looking through the movies. He eventually pulled out Santa Paws. "Ever seen the movie?" I asked him as I handed over the mug to him.

He shook his head. "Can't say that I have."

I laughed. "You are missing out on something then." I smiled. "It's really pretty cute." I then put my hand up to my mouth. "It's cute the first time. He's watched numerous times since the beginning of the month."

We laughed. "I love Christmas movies," Isaac stated. "It's another tradition with my family after we eat. Although, we put in a movie and get more food."

"I'm sorry... would you like another plate," I asked getting up to go and make him one.

"No, please sit. I'm fine. Thank you."

I sat back down as Jack started dancing around in excitement to watch the movie. Isaac chuckled and Jack put in the movie and it started. Isaac and I sat on the couch while Jack sat on the floor and we watched the movie. A few times I spotted Isaac chuckling right along with Jack and I considered what a nice guy he had to be to go along with this.

When the movie was done, Jack already said he wanted to watch another one, but I was quick to stop him. "Hold up! We need to give Isaac a chance to breathe." But Jack was way too excited.

"Coach Isaac what do you want to watch?" Jack asked already standing up and ready to put in the next movie.

"Can't we watch Elf?" Isaac asked, pleading with me right along with Jack. I couldn't believe that he just suggested Elf. I looked at him and I looked at Jack, realizing they were two peas in the pod.

"I'm game, but it is up to your Aunt," Isaac said waiting on a response.

I groaned playfully. "I can't say no to that face." I laughed and Jack jumped up and headed out of the living room. "Where are you going?" I asked.

"It's in my room," he said.

So, while he was gone I glanced at Isaac. "I bet this is more than you had in mind when I invited you."

He laughed. "It is great! I'm having a wonderful time." Even if he didn't mean it, it was nice that he would say that. We waited for what seemed like an eternity before I hollered up to see what was going on.

"Where are you?" I called out.

"I can't find it," he said. "Will you help me?"

I snickered and stood up. "We will be back!" I hurried from the room and ran up the stairs. I found Jack looking in a box and he had things scattered all around.

"I know it was in here," he said.

"I guess we can stream it," I replied.

He shook his head. "This is my mom's favorite." So, then I knew that we needed to at least try to find it. So, I helped him look in one box, then another, until we finally located it. He grabbed it and seemed excited to have found it and then we headed back downstairs.

"We found it..." I said heading back downstairs, but I stopped in my tracks when I found Isaac looking at something. In his hand was my journal. I hurried up to him and snatched it from his hands. "What are you doing?" I asked.

He looked dumbfounded. "I'm sorry. I accidentally knocked it off the table here, and I was putting it back."

"It looked like you were reading it," I said in an accusatory tone.

He shook his head. "I swear... I didn't see anything."

I could only imagine the thoughts running through his mind if he had read it and I didn't want to even know what he was thinking. Despite him telling me that he saw nothing, I felt that it was impossible to believe that. "I think you should go," I said.

He pleaded with me that he saw nothing, but I didn't want to hear it. I walked him to the door, and I heard Jack emotionally upset as he followed us. I couldn't even look at him as the irritation crowded my vision.

"I'm sorry," he said. "I swear, I didn't see anything." I looked away from him and he headed out the front door. "Thank you for today," he quietly stated.

I nodded and as he stepped off the front porch step, I shut the door and turned to Jack. He was looking as upset as I felt. I didn't want to kick him out, but he was holding my personal possession and the thought of him reading it was too hard to bear. "Go turn on the movie," he said. He tried to argue, but I said it again. "Go turn on the movie!"

He left the foyer, and I peeked out the front window to see Isaac pulling away from the house. A pit formed in my stomach realizing that I just may have overreacted.

❋

*I* waited for Jack to get to sleep before I grabbed my journal and opened it up. I had a lot to spill tonight, and I needed the quiet prayer time to do it in:

*Dear Future Husband,*

*Happy Thanksgiving! Today is a day when you can go over your blessings and for the most part, I did just that. Unfortunately, I found that it was also a difficult time because what started off being an amazing day, turned sour when I think I just kicked you out of the house. I got so scared when I saw you looking at my journal, I just assumed that you were reading it. It's true it was closed, but that didn't stop me from growing agitated at the mere thought. I don't know why I got so upset. Maybe I got scared of you reading I actually cared and did want something with you. Maybe I got scared that you would find that out and push me into it before I learned how to juggle Jack, work, and a love life. Everything is just so complicated now.*

*In hindsight, I feel I would have done things differently. I would have talked about it, to see if maybe I was being irrational. Yet, I barely said anything as you walked out the door. I wonder what you were thinking when you were driving home. I can only ask for forgiveness, but yet my stubbornness is blinding me to even do that. So, I stew over it and hope that one-day things will change and we can get past this and that you'll talk to me again.*

*You are a wonderful man. One that I would never imagine coming into my life without God's help. You treat Jack with so much respect and love that I can't picture you not being there for him and he's such a young child, but it's clear how much you mean to him. So, please forgive me for everything I have thought and know that if I was wrong about you, then I'm sorry.*

*I wonder why whenever I'm feeling ready and open to love, I let it slip away. I must be the problem, right?*

*Always and Forever,*
*Addison*

I needed to pray now. My heart was overwhelmed. I couldn't write any more after realizing that I was the problem, and I was using Jack as an excuse and now this journal.

*Father,*

*Forgive me and help Isaac to forgive me. Don't let my stupidity sour the happiness that could be between us. I pray what just happened today doesn't stop all that you have planned for me. I see some areas I need to change and help me to change it so that I can receive what you have for me.*

*I don't know what happened earlier today. I was just scared to rush into a relationship with things being so hectic in my life. Please lead him back to me, but until then I have to just hope for the best and hope that someday I will not be so quick to judge or misunderstand situations.*

I paused my prayer as Jack's scripture from earlier came to mind. I took out my journal and decided to write the entire scripture inside it:

*Love is patient, love is kind. It does not envy, it does not boast, it is not proud. It does not dishonor others, it is not self-seeking, it is not easily angered, it keeps no record of wrongs. Love does not delight in evil but rejoices with the truth. It always protects, always hopes, always perseveres.*
*1 Corinthians 13:4-7*

What stood out to me was the part of the scripture that said, 'it is not easily angered, it keeps no record of wrongs.'

*Father,*

*Help me not to be easily angered especially on stupid things like holding a journal that was actually possibly meant for him. Change my heart and my attitude. Make everything right again, please, Lord.*
*In Jesus' Name, Amen!*

It was a long day, so after writing the letter and saying my prayers, I closed up the journal and decided to go to bed. I hoped tomorrow would make things right for I was truly sorry.

# CHAPTER 14

*Another* month went by and it was the week before Christmas when I was at my office. I was fiddling around with my computer on my desk when I heard a knock at my door.

"Come in!" I called out, barely noticing who it was until I heard her voice.

"Hey, sis!"

I looked up and my eyes widened. "Brianna? Is that really you?" I jumped up from my desk and went to her. I pulled her into a hug, not able to at first yell at her like I wanted to. She'd kept me worried sick for nearly two-and-a-half months now. I should be scolding her, not hugging her, but all I could do was hold her in my arms. I felt tears stinging the backs of my eyes as I silently willed myself not to cry. Since she left, I had been making the same call to her that I had every day prior to that. It was a never-ending circle, and I never thought the day would come.

I finally pulled back and stared at her. "Where have you been?" I asked. Fear swept away, but I couldn't really take a full breath until we talked. "I've been worried sick." I then grabbed a hold of her shoulders and pushed her back. "You left your son!" That time my words were a little harsher.

She nodded each time. "I know and I'm sorry," she said. She even looked it, but I didn't want to let my guard down and act like any of this was all right, because it wasn't.

"Sorry doesn't cut it. You've abandoned your life... your son... what do you have to say for yourself?" I demanded.

She nodded and tears took over the corner of her eyes, making me go a little lighter on her. "I know you must hate me. I haven't returned any of your calls."

I heaved a sigh. "I don't hate you. You're my sister and I love you, but I've been worried sick. How have you been? Are you taking care of yourself? Where have you been?" I couldn't stop the questions from flying out of my mouth. I was overwhelmed with relief that she was there and I just wanted to know everything.

"I want to tell you all about it," she said. "But can you get away for lunch?" she asked.

I looked at my desk, which was overcrowded with papers, but there was no way I was going to pass up the opportunity to talk to her. I nodded. "Where do you want to go?"

"It doesn't matter. Wherever!"

I grabbed my purse and keys and was out the door and we were headed to a small café that was a couple of blocks away. I drove her because I was afraid to leave her out of my sight. On the way there, I attempted to get some information from her about what it was that she was going to talk to me about, but she wouldn't say anything, leaving me questioning really where she was for the past nearly three months.

I pulled into the café and we got out of the car and headed inside. We grabbed a seat in the corner and then the waitress came and got our drink orders, then she was gone. She looked at her menu and I didn't bother getting more information from her because I knew she would want to order before talking. And I was right. We both placed our order and the minute the waitress left the table, she started to talk.

"I got a job," she said.

That was amazing news. It was definitely something to lead off with and I was ecstatic for her. "Bri, that's awesome! I'm so happy. Where are you working?"

She hesitated for a moment before finally revealing that piece of the puzzle. "It's nearly three thousand miles away," she stated. "It's a small insurance company, and I started last month. They gave me time off for the holiday because I said I needed to come back and finalize some things."

"Wow! Nearly three thousand miles away? That's like on the other side of the country!" My mind was a blur, and I missed Jack already at the thought of them being so far away. I noted that she never offered where she was actually living, but it didn't matter at this rate. "So, I'm guessing that you'll be taking Jack with you soon?"

Brianna paused before saying anything. "Well, there's more to the story. A job isn't the only thing I've found. I found a man, and he's wonderful. I could potentially fall in love with him." She hesitated. "Not so sure he wants kids though."

When she said that, my face fell. "So, you're telling me that you're choosing this man over your son?" I asked. At that moment, our food came and I waited until the waitress dropped it off and left. When she did, I looked at her. "Please tell me that's not what you're saying!"

"I'm not saying that Addi," she said. "The truth is... I think Jack is better off with you. I'm sure he's happy." She paused and then asked, "Isn't he?"

I nodded. "That's not the point. You're his mother and a boy should be with his mother. I love him like he's my own, but it's not the same."

Even while I was arguing with her about how she should take Jack with her, I felt a pain shoot through my heart. I didn't want him to go, but I wanted to do what I thought would be best for him and I believed that could be Brianna.

"I've made up my mind Addi, and he deserves you to be his mother. I would be bringing him into a situation that I don't even know if he would belong. So, please... will you keep him?"

I couldn't believe my ears. How could a mother abandon her son like this again? "You're wrong Brianna. This is not how mother raised us."

"Oh, Addi, I'm not like you or momma. I can't raise him at a time like this. You don't want him to go to foster care, do you?"

I stopped eating and folded my arms across my chest. I was furious. I couldn't believe she had the thought of putting him into foster care if I didn't take him. Brianna saw the anger in my eyes and on my face. She looked down at her food avoiding eye contact with me. I thought about Jack and how he needed his mother. She couldn't see that. All she cared about were her wants and desires.

"He's not going to foster care!" I didn't need to even think on that. Of course I would take care of him. "I will take care of him!"

"Thank you! Thank you! Thank you!" she said over and over again. She was happy, but I wasn't. I wasn't happy because her decision would only hurt him. All I could do now was love him even more and bring him up in a loving home.

"I love you Brianna but I hope you come to your senses real quick."

She beamed. "I love you too!"

"And I want you to write that I have full custody of him so we have no trouble later on."

She nodded her head not even thinking about it and then went about eating her supper. I went about thinking how things could change so quickly. Jack was now permanently with me and I would happily raise him into the young man that I knew he could be. I just didn't want him to feel abandoned and so it would be tricky to explain it to a seven-year-old. I just needed some guidance from God and I would get that when I got home to pray.

❄

*I*t wasn't easy telling Brianna that I didn't think she should come around Jack while she was in town because I knew it would only confuse him, but she willingly accepted that deal and I said goodbye to her. Later that evening, I didn't tell Jack about my encounter with his mom the entire time while we ate supper. I was still looking for the right words to say and I still needed to have that conversation with God.

When he was tucked in bed and I kissed him goodnight, I left his room and went down to the living room. I grabbed my journal, but I didn't open it up. Instead, I closed my eyes and thought about Jack. I could see his smiling face when I closed my eyes and knew that he could count on me to be there for him always.

"God," I started. "I need you to help me through this. I don't know how I'm going to tell Jack about his mother, but he deserves to know the truth. Give me the wisdom and the words to prove to him that not everyone leaves. I will always be here for him and I don't want him to grow up thinking that he can't count on anyone. So, what can I tell him?" I paused and there was an overwhelming calmness that washed over me. I opened my eyes and looked up to the heavens and I knew that I just had to tell him. I had to speak from the heart.

I opened my journal and started off my letter:

*Dear Future Husband,*

*I never thought that I would see Brianna again. Of course I hoped that I would, but when she walked in my office today it was like all of my questions were answered over the past couple months. But a part of me was really sick about it because I knew if she was back, then chances were things were ending with Jack no longer staying here with me. It cut me to the core, because ever since he came to live with me, it is like I see a new meaning to life. I love that boy as much as I would love a son of mine.*

*But when she told me that she wasn't going to fight for me to get him back, I was shocked and appalled really, because what mother abandons their child not once... but twice. I just hope that he understands. I hope he doesn't take it too hard. I hope he knows that we're in this together and that I will never leave him.*

*How I wish that you were here too, to help me tell him. But I know that God will give me the words. He will provide me with exactly what I need to make this make sense to him. I have prayed about it and I will continue to pray about it until Jack knows the truth, but I won't say that he would be better off with Brianna, because it isn't true. I am his best shot now with happiness. Words don't fail me now. I will trust that with a lot of love for him,*

*I can prove that we are a powerhouse team and we'll get through whatever life throws our way.*

*Forever and Always,*
*Addison*

I closed my journal and leaned back in my chair. These last couple of months have been crazy. I sighed while closing my eyes and thought about Jack before drifting off to sleep and praying that all my words were in the truest form and that Jack would understand someway and somehow.

# CHAPTER 15

There's never a good time to share news with someone when you know it won't be what they want to hear. But I couldn't prolong it anymore. I had to tell Jack that his mom wasn't coming home now and most likely wouldn't be coming home later.

The next day, it was his last day of school, before they hit the almost two-week vacation. When we arrived home from school that afternoon, I felt so bad for not telling him sooner. Sure, I had only really learned of the news a few days earlier, but I should have confided the same day I learned. I just couldn't beat myself over that and Jack was excitedly talking about Christmas and how he couldn't wait to see what Santa brought him.

I was a little overwhelmed thinking about that myself, because frankly this was going to be hitting my purse hard and I didn't have a lot of extra money to run out and shower him with gifts until this big deal went through, but as he was talking about it, he said something that really stung me.

"Do you think Santa could bring me, Mommy, back?" he asked. I pulled into the driveway and parked the car and just sat there for a moment.

"Buddy, you and I need to have a little chat," I said.

He looked at me through the rearview mirror, but I motioned for him to go inside. We got inside the house and I grabbed his hand and led him to the living room. I took a deep breath and first off apologized.

"I'm sorry Jack if I don't do everything that is right by you. I only do my best and I want you to know that if you ever feel you're being mistreated or you have a question to ask me, you always can. Do you understand?" He nodded and so it began. "Your mom loves you very much. She told me so, and she wants to be the mom that you deserve. Unfortunately, she's hit some hard times, and she feels that you would be better off staying here and living with me... permanently." The words rushed out and he stared at me with a blank look on his face.

"Forever?" he quietly asked. "Will I see her again?"

I smiled. "Forever is a long time and I would like to believe that you will see her again. She just needs some space and I know that you are young and you might not understand that, but you have to know that this has nothing to do with you. This is all on her, buddy. So I don't want you thinking that you did anything wrong. Okay?"

He nodded and his eyes looked away from me. I felt like he had so many questions he wanted to ask me, and yet he was still too confused to get them out. "Can I call her?" he asked.

That was a question I hadn't anticipated him asking. Rightly so, he should be able to call his mom, but I knew it wasn't the right time. "Maybe someday soon. Let's just give her time. Can we do that?" He nodded slowly. "I love you!"

"I love you too!" he said, but his voice was so sad. I hugged him and then he let go. "I'm going to go clean my room up for Santa," he said.

I nodded. It was something that my own mom used to always tell me. She always mentioned how we needed to clean the room up for Santa to bring us new presents. I wondered if Brianna passed that down to him. I watched him as he hurried out of the room and ran up the stairs, undoubtedly still thinking about our conversation. I got up and busied myself with work and when supper came, I went up and got him. He was sound asleep and though he was asleep, I could tell he had been crying. It tore at me to know that he was crying himself to sleep over it.

I heaved a sigh and kissed him lightly on the forehead, then left his room. I expected him to wake up that night and say he was hungry, but when I went to bed, he had stayed in his room. I figured I would talk to him in the morning and make sure he was doing all right.

$\mathcal{T}$he next day it was Christmas Eve, and I went to the room to wake him for breakfast. I was sure he was starving. "Rise and shine sleepy head," I said turning on the lights.

I opened the door and was greeted by an empty bed. I walked over to the bed and tossed back his covers and looked around the room.

"Jack? Where are you?" I frantically ran around the second floor, checking out the bathroom and closets, then ran downstairs and checked to see if he was down there. He wasn't. I ran back upstairs to his bedroom and looked around to find clues and discovered that nothing was taken, but that still did nothing to ease my fears.

I ran downstairs as I dug my phone out of my pocket. I dialed up a number and waited for a response. "Hello?"

"Hey, it's Addison. I'm sorry to bother you, but Jack is gone."

"What do you mean he's gone?"

I could feel the tears stinging the back of my eyes. "He's gone! I woke up, and he's not here. I had a conversation with him and I don't think he liked it, but whatever the case... he's gone."

I started to shake and fear washed over me again. "It's going to be okay, Addison. He's seven. He couldn't have gone far. We'll find him. Wait for me there. I'll be right over."

I hung up, and it hit me. I didn't even remember dialing his number, but it seemed like my first instinct was to call up Isaac. I didn't know why my mind would go there when I should have called the police, but I figured he couldn't have gone far. We'll search for him first before we called.

I waited at the door for Isaac to arrive and he only took ten minutes to get there. When he got inside, he wrapped me up in a hug.

"We'll find him, Addison. I have no doubt. Come on!" I locked up the house and headed for his vehicle where he would drive us around to check out places where Jack might have wound up.

I was trembling as we took that drive. At one point, he reached over and touched my hand and whispered that everything was going to be all right. It was easy for him to say, but while we checked out places he might have gone, the possibilities were growing smaller. We went to the school gym, we checked out every friend's house that he could wander off too. We stopped by several of the neighbor's homes to see if he was there. Every place we checked, we were left empty-handed.

We rode around for three hours, with not a sign of him. "It's so cold out," I said.

He squeezed my hand. "I'm sure he's where it's warm," he encouraged me.

He was comforting me, and I appreciated that, but I felt hopeless. I closed my eyes and said a silent prayer. *"Lord, please lead me to where he is. He needs me. I need him. Help me find him."*

I opened my eyes, and it was as if a bolt of lightning flashed in my mind. "I know where he is," I said.

"Where is he?" he asked. I glanced at him and led him right to the location that was weighing heavily on my mind.

❄

*We* pulled into the parking lot of Brianna's apartment building. He gave me a curious look, but we parked and then jumped out of the vehicle and ran towards where the Holy Spirit was leading me to. We got up the stairs to her apartment and sure enough at the doorstep was Jack.

I heaved a sigh of relief and ran to him. "Jack!" I called out.

He looked up and his face was a mess. He had been crying and tears streaked his cheeks. I pulled him into a hug, too worried to do anything like scold him. I was so relieved to even see him. "I was so worried about you," I cried.

"I'm sorry," his muffled voice came out.

I pulled back from him. "What are you doing here?" I asked.

He started to sob again, and I pulled him into my lap. Isaac stayed at the top of the stairs and just watched us as I talked to him.

"I thought if I could get to Mommy she would come and stay with us for Christmas. I got here, and she wasn't here, so I didn't know what else to do."

"Buddy... I wish that you could be with your Mommy too. I really do. She's just not able to be here for you like a Mommy should and that's why she enlisted my help to help her out. Your Mommy would be here for you, but she has some things that she has to take care of. You have to believe that."

"I don't want to leave you, Aunt Addison. I love being with you, but I thought we could all just be together."

My heart melted for him and I pulled him into a hug. At that point, the bond between us strengthened and I couldn't imagine what would happen if I ever lost him. "I love you, buddy," she said, kissing him on the cheek. "Let's go home?"

He nodded, and a smile appeared on his lips. As we headed towards the stairs, he spotted Isaac and his face lit up. "What are you doing here?" he asked.

"I came to make sure everything was all right with you. You gave us quite a scare, buddy," he said rubbing his head.

The three of us walked down the stairs and headed back to Isaac's vehicle. As we walked out to his car, I felt love for both men creep into my heart. I smiled at Isaac as he held the door open for me, then I mouthed the words, thank you! He nodded and then I got into his vehicle as Jack got situated in the backseat. I glanced at the back seat and smiled at him. His face was still splotchy, but he looked like things were going to improve for him, or at least I hoped they would.

Isaac and I kept tossing glances to one another as we made the way back to my house. When we pulled onto our street, I heard soft snoring and I looked in the backseat to find that Jack was asleep. It had to have been a long day for him already and I wondered what time it was when he left the house. "He's asleep," I said.

He laughed. "Poor guy must be tired!"

He parked the car in the driveway and we got out. He walked around and unbuckled him from the backseat, then picked him up in his arms and carried him to the front door. I unlocked it and let him in and then led the way up the stairs to Jack's bedroom. He laid him down on the bed and then we left his room and I shut the door, so it was just ajar. As Isaac walked behind me another feeling rushed through me. I couldn't shake it any longer.

## CHAPTER 16

*I* glanced at my watch as we headed downstairs. It was just after one and we were missing lunch, but I wasn't even hungry. I was still on an adrenaline high to locate Jack and thanks to Isaac he was found and unscathed. We walked to the living room, and I sat down breathing a sigh of relief that that nightmare was over. "I don't know how I can ever repay you," I said.

He shrugged it off with a wave of his hand. "You don't need to repay me. I was happy to be here and I would do it again and again in a heartbeat." He paused and frowned. "Well, I really hope I don't have to do it again, but I'll be here if need be. That's the point I'm trying to point out."

I laughed. "I get it."

In that moment, I just wanted to enjoy his company and not have to worry about any other problems, but I also needed someone to talk to and Isaac was the one I felt most comfortable telling my problems to.

"I don't want to come across as complaining," I started. "I have truly been blessed the past few months with getting Jack and all, but it has been a stressful time and I feel that I have pushed you away because I didn't know how to balance it all."

I could admit that to him now. I was terrified of getting too close to something that could potentially be amazing, only to have it blown up in my face.

"I get that," he said. I looked at him and his genuine smile proved that he did.

I looked to the right where the Christmas tree stood. "This is going to be a lousy Christmas for him. I only could get him one thing which was the video game he wanted. I just feel that I'll let him down because I haven't gotten him more gifts."

"You could never do that," he said. He reached over and touched my hand and I tried to force a smile. "You are a good person and you care for him. The greatest gift is being able to care for him like you have been doing. Anyone can see that. It's not about what you provide as far as gifts go."

"But he's seven and still believes in Santa Claus. I don't want to let him down."

"You won't," he said, trying to assure me. "Trust me! This is going to be his and your best Christmas yet."

I wanted to believe that, but I had so many doubts going through my mind. "I hope you're right!" I said.

He smiled and stood up. "I should probably get going. It's already been an exhausting day for you and it's only barely beginning. Plus, I have to get ready for service tonight," he said.

I smiled and stood up and walked him to the door. At the doorway, he turned to face me. I couldn't let him leave without saying that I was sorry. So, I blurted it out.

"I'm sorry for what happened on Thanksgiving. I'm sorry for pushing you away."

He nodded his head accepting the apology and then he smiled. "Love is patient, remember?"

My heart skipped a beat as I thought about those words and the scripture that I had written that day in my journal.

"Yes, it irritated and annoyed me but I realized that you were scared and trying to figure things out. I realized that you had Jack and his best interest at heart and I knew that if God said that you're the one for me then I have to have long-suffering love until He changed your heart and made you understand the love and care that I have for you. It may seem crazy but you can kick me out one hundred times and I'll still be standing in there with you like today. Love is patient. Love is long passion. My love for you in this short time has a long fuse. Love has no limits. I was willing to step away and give you space because I knew God would speak to your heart and you would come around."

My eyes started to water as he expressed those words to me and to my surprise he reached up and caressed my cheek with his hand. Our eyes met before he moved in and brushed a kiss on my lips as we stood underneath the mistletoe. I felt like the luckiest woman in the world and as we parted, he continued to glow.

"I want to be by your side, Addison. If you have me, I would love to help you raise Jack. We belong together and I know you feel it too."

"Like a gift from God!" We said the words in unison and I smiled.

"I want that too, Isaac," I finally admitted. We again kissed and the walls around my heart completely shattered. "Spend Christmas with us tomorrow morning"

He nodded. "I'll be here. Goodbye, my dear Addison."

He opened up the door and walked out and I waved to him from the porch. I smiled as he got into his vehicle and drove away. So far this was the best Christmas yet and I could feel it would only get better.

❄

Once Jack woke up, things between us seemed to be even better. I made it my vow not to tell him how worried I was that he left because the important thing was that he wasn't hurt and that we found him before too much time could pass. The sleep did him good, and he seemed to gravitate even more towards me and I didn't want to add a conflict between us.

We ate supper, and I then looked at him. "Want to go to the Christmas Eve service at church?" I asked. When this had all happened, I was going to just let him relax for the rest of the day, but he seemed to be in good spirits and eagerly agreed that he wanted to go. We got dressed and headed out to the church in time to get there a little early and spend time greeting some parishioners. As we entered, the greeters were smiling with a cheer. "Merry Christmas!"

I smiled and gave the same greeting back to them as did Jack. Several people were milling around the church near the sanctuary doors, so we waved and smiled to several people we knew, hollering out greetings such as Good evening and Merry Christmas to you!

"Addison! Jack!" I looked at Jack and smiled when I heard Isaac calling out our names. I didn't know if he would be there, but I was hoping he would be. I turned around and saw him hurrying up to us. "How are you guys doing? I didn't expect you here tonight. You only showed up because you knew I was coming," he said smiling and remembering the time I accused him of only coming to church because I was there.

I felt so silly, but I was glad that I could laugh about it now. "We're doing well. How about you?"

He couldn't have been smiling any wider like he was a man in love and I loved the fact that I was the one that put that smile on his face. "Couldn't be better," he said. "Would you like to go in?" he asked.

The three of us entered the sanctuary, and I felt like a true family as we went into the service together. We took a seat at the spot that I usually sat and I was in the middle. On one side, Jack was holding my hand, and on the other, Isaac took my hand in his. I glanced at him and he looked at me in a loving and passionate way that you would find in the movies. I kept thinking how at any moment I would wake up from this dream but it wasn't a dream, it was finally a reality.

Jack leaned forward and started talking to Isaac about basketball. I looked at the two in conversation and everything just fell into place. When the music started playing, and the choir started singing, Jack moved back and we all stood up to see the dancers that were dancing and hear the Christmas Carol that was being sung by the choir.

The Christmas Eve Service was nice in that there was lots of music, laughter, and fellowship. As we were nearing the end of the service, they sent around candles and then the song Silent Night started playing as one by one, they sent flames down our aisles so that the whole sanctuary was filled with lights while we sang. It was a beautiful sight and brought tears to my eyes. I looked in the flame as we sang through the chorus and I rejoiced in everything that Christ had already given me that Christmas. I knew that for the first time everything was just right in my life.

When the song came to an end, we all blew out the candles and I looked up at Isaac. He was beaming from ear to ear. I could tell this was his best Christmas yet too. We left our aisle and headed out of the sanctuary and Isaac fell into step with us once service was over.

"What time in the morning should I be there to open presents tomorrow?" he asked.

"Four!" Jack hollered out.

Isaac laughed. "Well, if you wake up that early, how do you know that Santa had time to get your presents all ready for you?" he asked.

When Isaac said that, I felt a pit in my stomach form. I only had the time and money to get him one thing and this was going to be a meager Christmas for him, no doubt. Jack just frowned. "How about five?"

I chuckled as he said that. "Let's make it eight. What do you say?"

He looked disappointed but nodded. I looked at Isaac and he was still grinning, but then it dawned on me that I didn't buy him anything because I didn't know we would finally find our way to one another.

We walked to the door, and it wasn't until we got there that we noticed the gathering of people outside as they all were engrossed in watching something.

"What's going on?" Isaac wondered aloud. We stepped outside, and that's when we noticed the snow that was coming down. It was truly a Christmas blessing in the making and Jack started eagerly jumping up and down. We didn't think it would be a White Christmas, but at the rate of the snow already piling up, it was looking like it just might be.

"Wow!" I breathlessly gasped at the beauty of it all and I heard Isaac next to me.

"I know.... so beautiful." When I looked at him, he was looking at me. I blushed and then turned back to the snow that was falling. It surely was beautiful. It was everything I could hope for this Christmas. I loved this time of year.

✳

*J*ack was way too excited to want to get to bed, but I kept telling him that he needed to go to bed because there was going to be a busy day ahead for us. I tried to steer clear of mentioning the presents because I didn't want another round of disappointment from me. So finally he agreed, and I said goodnight and left his room.

I walked down into the living room and grabbed my journal and then went over to the couch where I curled up in front of the fire that was still burning in the fireplace. I took out my pen and wrote the letter:

*Dear Isaac,*

*It was you. All this time it was you and I was here pushing you away. So much time was wasted because of me being scared. Scared of what? I don't even know.*

*I am so grateful for your words on being patient. It settled so much in my heart. I thank God for Jack because if it wasn't for Jack, you and I wouldn't have met. Thank you for hanging in there. Thank you for showing me that you are here for me... you were here for us.*

*When Jack came up missing, I thought of only you. You were the one that I was trusting with my heart to find him. You were the one that I wanted by my side to look for him. You are the one that I want in my life, forever and always. And this Christmas, God has truly given me the gift of love. How could anyone turn away from that?*

*You have so much goodness in your heart and it is everything that I have been dreaming of and looking for since I was a little girl. When I started writing these letters, all along I was writing them to you and I didn't even know it. You were even back then shaping up to be the man that I would fall in love with. God had this plan from the minute we were* born to get us together. It just took me by surprise when it actually happened at what seemed like the wrong time for me but in all actuality, it was the right time. God set this whole thing up for us to meet. It amazes me!

And you say that you want to be by my side and help raise Jack and I say yes. I want you here next to me for all of our days. I can't imagine a life without you, now that we have finally found our way to one another. So, just ask me the question and I will always say yes.

Forever and always I will love you,

Addison

I read the letter once more, and I smiled because it was perfect. Now, it was time for prayer.

Father,

Thank you for this winter of romance. Thank you for sending Isaac my way. Thank you even for Brianna leaving Jack with me. Thank you for setting it up this way. I may not have understood it all in the beginning but now I really know that all things work together for good to them that love God, to them who are the called according to his purpose. I see this verse ever so present in my life and I thank you.

This single season may have been a long wait but looking back, it was worth it. I've grown so much and I've developed a relationship with you. That's the most important part. You've taught me so much and loved me so much and I am forever grateful.

Now, because of You ordering my steps, I finally get to spend it with someone special. It was all because I waited on You and all because I trusted You that I have someone special. I even developed a deeper relationship with You too and because I have a relationship with you it allowed for Isaac to come into my life and notice me. Having a relationship with you was necessary for Isaac to find me.

Thank you also for helping me to face my fears. Here I was praying for a husband and You sent him but I almost sent him away. I thank You for keeping him and having him love me past my stupid fears. For I should have remembered the scripture verse where it said, 'For God has not given us a *spirit of fear but of power and love and self-control! Thank you for helping me get over my fear and thank you for bringing me to this place of love.*

*Thank you for giving me love too. I will cherish what you have given me and I will love whole heartily just like the way You love us. I won't ever take it for granted.*

*I love you and You will always be my first love. As I come out of this single season, I will always put You first. You've been there when no one else was and I will never forget your loving kindness and how Your love never failed. One thing has remained through it all is that your love is constant and I thank you for that as Isaac and I enter into a new chapter that we are reminded of your love and how constant it is. Help us to always be reminded of Your example of love that goes on and on and even outlasts the energizer bunny. May our love be so deep just as Your love is so deep and so wide for us.*

*Once again, I love you, forever and always and in Jesus' Name, I pray, Amen!*

I couldn't wait until Christmas morning. I suddenly was feeling like a little kid that was too excited to sleep. The only difference was, my excitement was to see Isaac, and I was ready for our story to be read since God had already written it. This was going to be a beautiful story to read. It was all unfolding. There's never a good time to share the news with someone when you know it won't be what they want to hear. But I couldn't prolong it anymore. I had to tell Jack that his mom wasn't coming home now and most likely wouldn't be coming home later.

The next day, it was his last day of school, before they hit the almost two-week vacation. When we arrived home from school that afternoon, I felt so bad for not telling him sooner. Sure, I had only really learned of the news a few days earlier, but I should have confided the same day I learned. I just couldn't beat myself over that and Jack was excitedly talking about Christmas and how he couldn't wait to see what Santa brought him.

I was a little overwhelmed thinking about that myself, because frankly this was going to be hitting my purse hard and I didn't have a lot of extra money to run out and shower him with gifts until this big deal went through, but as he was talking about it, he said something that really stung me.

"Do you think Santa could bring me, Mommy, back?" he asked. I pulled into the driveway and parked the car and just sat there for a moment.

"Buddy, you and I need to have a little chat," I said.

He looked at me through the rearview mirror, but I motioned for him to go inside. We got inside the house and I grabbed his hand and led him to the living room. I took a deep breath and first off apologized.

"I'm sorry Jack if I don't do everything that is right by you. I only do my best and I want you to know that if you ever feel you're being mistreated or you have a question to ask me, you always can. Do you understand?" He nodded and so it began. "Your mom loves you very much. She told me so, and she wants to be the mom that you deserve. Unfortunately, she's hit some hard times, and she feels that you would be better off staying here and living with me... permanently." The words rushed out and he stared at me with a blank look on his face.

"Forever?" he quietly asked. "Will I see her again?"

I smiled. "Forever is a long time and I would like to believe that you will see her again. She just needs some space and I know that you are young and you might not understand that, but you have to know that this has nothing to do with you. This is all on her, buddy. So I don't want you thinking that you did anything wrong. Okay?"

He nodded and his eyes looked away from me. I felt like he had so many questions he wanted to ask me, and yet he was still too confused to get them out. "Can I call her?" he asked.

That was a question I hadn't anticipated him asking. Rightly so, he should be able to call his mom, but I knew it wasn't the right time. "Maybe someday soon. Let's just give her time. Can we do that?" He nodded slowly. "I love you!"

"I love you too!" he said, but his voice was so sad. I hugged him and then he let go. "I'm going to go clean my room up for Santa," he said.

I nodded. It was something that my own mom used to always tell me. She always mentioned how we needed to clean the room up for

Santa to bring us new presents. I wondered if Brianna passed that down to him. I watched him as he hurried out of the room and ran up the stairs, undoubtedly still thinking about our conversation. I got up and busied myself with work and when supper came, I went up and got him. He was sound asleep and though he was asleep, I could tell he had been crying. It tore at me to know that he was crying himself to sleep over it.

I heaved a sigh and kissed him lightly on the forehead, then left his room. I expected him to wake up that night and say he was hungry, but when I went to bed, he had stayed in his room. I figured I would talk to him in the morning and make sure he was doing all right.

*T*he next day it was Christmas Eve, and I went to the room to wake him for breakfast. I was sure he was starving. "Rise and shine sleepy head," I said turning on the lights.

I opened the door and was greeted by an empty bed. I walked over to the bed and tossed back his covers and looked around the room.

"Jack? Where are you?" I frantically ran around the second floor, checking out the bathroom and closets, then ran downstairs and checked to see if he was down there. He wasn't. I ran back upstairs to his bedroom and looked around to find clues and discovered that nothing was taken, but that still did nothing to ease my fears.

I ran downstairs as I dug my phone out of my pocket. I dialed up a number and waited for a response. "Hello?"

"Hey, it's Addison. I'm sorry to bother you, but Jack is gone."

"What do you mean he's gone?"

I could feel the tears stinging the back of my eyes. "He's gone! I woke up, and he's not here. I had a conversation with him and I don't think he liked it, but whatever the case... he's gone."

I started to shake and fear washed over me again. "It's going to be okay, Addison. He's seven. He couldn't have gone far. We'll find him. Wait for me there. I'll be right over."

I hung up, and it hit me. I didn't even remember dialing his number, but it seemed like my first instinct was to call up Isaac. I didn't know why my mind would go there when I should have called the police, but I figured he couldn't have gone far. We'll search for him first before we called.

I waited at the door for Isaac to arrive and he only took ten minutes to get there. When he got inside, he wrapped me up in a hug. "We'll find him, Addison. I have no doubt. Come on!" I locked up the house and headed for his vehicle where he would drive us around to check out places where Jack might have wound up.

I was trembling as we took that drive. At one point, he reached over and touched my hand and whispered that everything was going to be all right. It was easy for him to say, but while we checked out places he might have gone, the possibilities were growing smaller. We went to the school gym, we checked out every friend's house that he could wander off too. We stopped by several of the neighbor's homes to see if he was there. Every place we checked, we were left empty-handed.

We rode around for three hours, with not a sign of him. "It's so cold out," I said.

He squeezed my hand. "I'm sure he's where it's warm," he encouraged me.

He was comforting me, and I appreciated that, but I felt hopeless. I closed my eyes and said a silent prayer. "*Lord, please lead me to where he is. He needs me. I need him. Help me find him.*"

I opened my eyes, and it was as if a bolt of lightning flashed in my mind. "I know where he is," I said.

"Where is he?" he asked. I glanced at him and led him right to the location that was weighing heavily on my mind.

❄

*W*e pulled into the parking lot of Brianna's apartment building. He gave me a curious look, but we parked and then jumped out of the vehicle and ran towards where the Holy Spirit was leading me to. We got up the stairs to her apartment and sure enough at the doorstep was Jack.

I heaved a sigh of relief and ran to him. "Jack!" I called out.

He looked up and his face was a mess. He had been crying and tears streaked his cheeks. I pulled him into a hug, too worried to do anything like scold him. I was so relieved to even see him. "I was so worried about you," I cried.

"I'm sorry," his muffled voice came out.

I pulled back from him. "What are you doing here?" I asked.

He started to sob again, and I pulled him into my lap. Isaac stayed at the top of the stairs and just watched us as I talked to him.

"I thought if I could get to Mommy she would come and stay with us for Christmas. I got here, and she wasn't here, so I didn't know what else to do."

"Buddy... I wish that you could be with your Mommy too. I really do. She's just not able to be here for you like a Mommy should and that's why she enlisted my help to help her out. Your Mommy would be here for you, but she has some things that she has to take care of. You have to believe that."

"I don't want to leave you, Aunt Addison. I love being with you, but I thought we could all just be together."

My heart melted for him and I pulled him into a hug. At that point, the bond between us strengthened and I couldn't imagine what would happen if I ever lost him. "I love you, buddy," she said, kissing him on the cheek. "Let's go home?"

He nodded, and a smile appeared on his lips. As we headed towards the stairs, he spotted Isaac and his face lit up. "What are you doing here?" he asked.

"I came to make sure everything was all right with you. You gave us quite a scare, buddy," he said rubbing his head.

The three of us walked down the stairs and headed back to Isaac's vehicle. As we walked out to his car, I felt love for both men creep into my heart. I smiled at Isaac as he held the door open for me, then I mouthed the words, thank you! He nodded and then I got into his vehicle as Jack got situated in the backseat. I glanced at the back seat and smiled at him. His face was still splotchy, but he looked like things were going to improve for him, or at least I hoped they would.

Isaac and I kept tossing glances to one another as we made the way back to my house. When we pulled onto our street, I heard soft snoring and I looked in the backseat to find that Jack was asleep. It had to have been a long day for him already and I wondered what time it was when he left the house. "He's asleep," I said.

He laughed. "Poor guy must be tired!"

He parked the car in the driveway and we got out. He walked around and unbuckled him from the backseat, then picked him up in his arms and carried him to the front door. I unlocked it and let him in and then led the way up the stairs to Jack's bedroom. He laid him down in the bed and then we left his room and I shut the door, so it was just ajar. As Isaac walked behind me another feeling rushed through me. I couldn't shake it any longer.

# CHAPTER 17

now was still falling outside when we woke up the next morning. I got up and got dressed, but told Jack he could stay in his pajamas. He was playing in his room when I heard the doorbell and I knew that the glorious day was getting ready to begin. I went to the door and opened it and my jaw dropped. There was Isaac standing in my doorway, holding a bunch of wrapped presents in his arms and covered in snow. He held a goofy grin on his face and I was beside myself.

"What's going on?" I asked, holding the door open for him to get inside.

He laughed as he entered and then leaned in to kiss me as we were once again under the mistletoe. "I just did a little late shopping yesterday. Hope you don't mind." He winked at me and my heart grew fuller in that moment.

"Thank you, Isaac!"

I closed the door but noticed his car wasn't out front.

"Where's your car?"

He shrugged his shoulders. "I had to walk here. They haven't plowed the streets as you can see and it is just too dangerous to drive but I had to get here to give you these gifts."

He smiled and headed off to the living room where he put the presents under the tree. I couldn't believe he made his way through the snow just to get here to be with me and Jack. I stood amazed at his thoughtfulness and I stared at the tree that now had way more presents than I had ever seen under one of my trees before. I wiped away a tear that was threatening to show up, then walked over to the stairs. "Jack... Coach Isaac is here."

That was all I needed to say as he came running down the stairs and bypassed me to get to the living room. I nearly fell over as he rushed towards the Christmas tree but thank God Isaac was there to catch me as we both laughed.

"Whoa!" I heard him exclaim, and we chuckled at Jacks excitement.

Whether he knew where the presents came from, I'm not sure, but he didn't seem as interested in them at the moment, as he did in greeting Isaac. Their relationship was truly an amazing love for one another and I knew Isaac would make the perfect life partner to help me with that.

They were laughing with one another as Isaac handed him a present and he tore into it. He got so many things that were right up his alley and it was like Isaac knew what to get. I walked over and took a seat on the couch and watched them, not able to interrupt the excitement before me. But when Jack handed me a gift that was under the tree, I looked at him and then glanced at Isaac.

"I didn't get you anything," I said, whispering to Isaac.

He got up off the floor and took a seat on the couch. "You're wrong. You gave me so much this Christmas. You and Jack are all I need."

I smiled but still felt like I wished I could have given him something. I opened up the small box and my eyes widened when I saw what was inside. I looked at him and he got off the couch and knelt in front of me.

"You have no idea the gift that you are to me." I looked off and saw that Jack was watching us. The smile on his face was infectious, and I turned back to Isaac. "I meant everything I said. I want to be with you through this and so will you marry me?"

I looked at the ring that sparkled before me. I didn't waste another minute as I quickly nodded with tears that couldn't help but fall. He removed the ring out of the box and put it on my finger and we gently kissed. Jack jumped up and ran over to us and hugged us as we each laughed.

"Let's get back to those presents, I said. Jack went back to under the tree and Isaac rejoined him on the floor. I stood up and moved away from them and watched from afar.

I closed my eyes and said my thanks to God.

"God, you have given me the greatest gift and you're right... that gift is love. Thank you for bringing me a man to love me wholeheartedly and love Jack just as much," I said praying within my heart.

I opened my eyes and saw Jack and Isaac playing with some of his new found toys and I knew what gift I could give Isaac. But I needed to do it when it was just the two of us.

So, I waited for that. We had breakfast and then I could tell that Jack was eagerly champing at the bit to get back to playing with his toys. "Hey, buddy... want to take some of your toys upstairs?" I asked.

"Yeah! Of course I do!" he jumped up from the kitchen table and went back to the living room, loaded up his arms and hurried up the stairs. I turned to Isaac and motioned for him to get up and follow me.

"You have truly made this Christmas neither one of us is going to forget," I said as we headed back into the living room.

"I'm glad I could," he replied.

I grabbed the journal from the hiding place and he looked at it, surely remembering it was the book that got him into trouble on Thanksgiving.

"Since I was young, I've been envisioning what my future husband would be like and every morning I say a prayer for him and every night, I write a letter to him. I keep these letters and prayers in this journal. When I thought you were going to see them, I was worried that you would judge me or think it was stupid. I had to make sure you were the one. No one else has ever seen these letters until now!" I handed the journal to him and he looked at me.

"Are you sure?" he asked. "I don't want you kicking me out again."

I playfully hit him with the journal and continued, "Sometime ago, I realized it was you and I've been writing them to you this whole time, so it is high-time you finally read them. Merry Christmas!"

I stepped back as he took a seat on the couch and opened up the journal to day one. I didn't want to watch him as he was reading them, so I made myself scarce and headed up the stairs to find Jack.

He was on his bed playing with a robot when I got inside his room. He looked up. "Hey, Aunt Addison, look!" He was showing me what it could do, and I nodded and smiled at him, then went over and sat next to him.

"Do you like all your presents?" I asked.

He nodded. "I do, but..." His words trailed off when he put his robot down and looked at me.

"What's wrong?" I asked.

"Everything's great, but my present is you."

When he said that I tilted my head, unable to control the urge to get all emotional again. "Buddy..." I pulled him closer, and we hugged. "My gift is you too! I love you so much!"

"I love you too!"

We parted, and I was the luckiest aunt on the planet because I realized that it wasn't about the presents for him as I worried, it was about him having someone to love him and I would provide that love. As long as he was taken care of, then he would be satisfied.

I heard a knock on the door and I looked up to find Isaac. I frowned. "You can't be done already," I said, then laughed as I stood up and went to him.

He had the journal in his hand. "I have more to read, but I just read the last one you wrote last night. It's beautiful. It's a confirmation and I'm never going to let you or Jack down. I love you!"

I smiled. "And I love you!"

Without any worries or doubts, we were going to be a family. This was our time to be happy and nothing could come between that. We would be together forever and always. It was a winter romance that only God could write. I was forever grateful for the wait. I was forever grateful for a winter of romance.

*Thank you God for always coming through forever and always!*

# PRAYERS

God has a beautiful love story that he is preparing for you. Here you will find all the prayers that were in the book and more prayers for you to pray. If you're seeking God's best these prayers will encourage your heart, build your faith, and uplift you. Prayer and fasting is the key to unlocking the love story God is preparing for you. Take these prayers and the prayers throughout the book to pray for your future husband to pray for yourself.

# PRAYER FOR A DEEPER RELATIONSHIP WITH GOD

*Father, I love You with everything that is within me. You are such an amazing God that my desire is to be closer to You. I pray starting today that I will be taken into a deeper relationship with You. I believe that You want me to come closer to You. I want to walk with You as those in the Bible walked with You. I desire and need a deeper relationship with You. In this season, help our relationship to grow deeper and stronger. Help me to seek Your face.*

*My heart's desire is to dwell with You and only You. For You are the one I truly need. You are the one I really want. Draw me closer and closer. Help me to study Your word more. Help me to pray more. Help me to fast more. Help me to need You and only You more in this season.*

*Open my eyes, that I may behold wonderful things from Your law (**Psalms 119:18**). Open my eyes so that I may see You.*

*I pray that I will grow and hear that still small voice and that I will be attentive to Your call and voice. Be with me Father, and take me to new levels in You. Help me to continue to hunger and thirst for You. Fill me up because I just want more of You.*

*Help me to seek Your face and not Your hand. As I seek Your*
*face take me to new levels in You. My desire is to take steps*
*closer to You daily. Even now Father, bring someone near*
*to me who has already come to know You, walked with You*
*and has a deeper relationship with You so that they can*
*help me to grow and to know Your Word even more.*
*Father, I want to commit and make a daily habit of confessing*
*my sins to You, listening to You when You speak, speaking*
*to You through prayer, finding other believers who desire*
*to be closer to You, have regular church attendance, and be*
*obedient to You in everything including my dating life. I*
*know that as I make this commitment I will draw closer to*
*You and have that deeper relationship You and I both*
*desire. Day and night I will seek You.*
*In Jesus' Name, Amen!*

❋

## NOTES

_____

_____

_____

_____

_____

_____

_____

_____

_____

_____

# PRAYER FOR GOD TO WRITE YOUR LOVE STORY

⨳

*Father, I give You permission to write my love story. I*
*understand that what I see on television or read in books*
*are nothing compared to what You have and can do*
*for me.*
*Father, I let go because what You have and what You are*
*writing is greater than what I can come up with. I*
*surrender and I give You the pen so that You can have*
*Your way and write the love story that is meant to be. I*
*tear up the pages I have already written and I am giving*
*You permission to write a whole new story.*
*Father, as I wait for the book to be completed and given to me,*
*help me not to be impatient. Help me not to write*
*something myself. Help me not to be desperate but to trust*
*that You have the fairytale and life, I've always imagined*
*and dreamed of.*
*Help me not to look at someone else's story when You finally*
*do give it to me. Help me to see that my story, my book is*
*perfect in every way too. Help me to understand that every*
*person's story will be different. Let me not be envious. Let*

*me not compare. Let me not try to emulate another
person's story. Help me to be content with my own story.
Father, write my love story and help me to enjoy the pages You
have already written for me. I trust and rely on You. For
You have the perfect cover, the perfect binding, the perfect
pages and the perfect words for my story. I'm excited and I
can wait to receive and read the love story You've written
for me but also help me to remember that the greatest love
story ever was You dying on the cross for me.
In Jesus' Name, Amen!*

❄

## NOTES

---------------------------------------------
---------------------------------------------
---------------------------------------------
---------------------------------------------
---------------------------------------------
---------------------------------------------
---------------------------------------------
---------------------------------------------
---------------------------------------------
---------------------------------------------
---------------------------------------------
---------------------------------------------
---------------------------------------------
---------------------------------------------
---------------------------------------------
---------------------------------------------

# PRAYER FOR A BROKEN HEART

⮾

*F*ather, in Your word You said, to Come to Me, all You who are weary and burdened, and I will give You rest **(Matthew 11:28)**.

*I come to You admitting that I need rest. My heart is broken. I've been hurt. I feel rejected and ashamed. I've given my heart to one too many and I need You to heal the wounds that I am carrying. I have nothing but hurt left, and it doesn't seem to want to go away. I feel so broken and my heart is torn apart. I am crushed. The pain of the past consumes me.*

*Now, I bring to You my burdens. I bring to You the pain of the past. You know what I've gone through. You know I can't make it without You and so I need You to comfort my heart and help me to move on.*

*Your word says that You are close to the brokenhearted (**Psalm 34:18**). Lord, I need You to be ever so close to me. Wrap Your arms around me. Let Your love cloud every doubt, every fear, and mend this broken heart. Comfort me and* *help me find hope again. Comfort me and help me find peace again.*

*Father, I ask that You give me the strength to let go of the past and let go of these hurts and pains. Help me to remember that it is better to trust in You than to find confidence in man (Psalm 118:8).*

*I am asking You to break down the walls that I have built up because of the hurts and pains inside of me. Tear them down so that I can be free again. Heal my heart and put the pieces back together again. Transform me and make me whole and ready to love again.*

*Father, heal me completely. Heal me of whatever might separate me from You. Heal my memory. Heal my heart. Heal my emotions. Let there be freedom!*

*I give You the pieces of my heart right now. Heal this broken heart, in Jesus' Name, Amen.*

**Take this time to talk to God about all the hurts You have. Write it down or speak it out to God. Tell all that has hurt You and allow God to fix each piece one by one.**

❄

NOTES

_____
_____
_____
_____
_____
_____
_____
_____
_____

# PRAYER FOR BEING CONTENT

*Father, in this season of my life, help me to be like Paul and to learn that in whatever situation I am in to be content* (**Philippians 4:11**). *Lord, I pray You will help me to be content and help me to know that I have everything I need in You.*

*Father, I pray for peace and joy in all circumstances. Help me not to complain but to leap for joy in it all. Thank You for helping me to remember that You provide for me and that at this moment I have everything that I need. Lord, help me to get rid of the years of discontentment and help me to have the joy of the Lord. Help me to focus on You and not on what I think I don't have.*

*I ask that You take me through the school of contentment and help me to pass with flying colors. I ask that You help me to appreciate and focus on all the good things that I have already.*

*Father, I do have a need, and that need is to be married. While I am waiting for You to move show me how to smile and show me how to be happy. Help me to be content with my life and to remind myself that everything is good and that*

*I can rejoice while I wait. Show me even the little things in*
*my life now that I can rejoice and be content about.*
*Help me to stop comparing my life to others. Help me to*
*realize that since I am in You, my grass is just as green.*
*Lord, I praise You and I am very grateful for all You have*
*done already. You have done so much for me already and*
*one thing I can thank You for right now is that my name is*
*in the Lamb's Book of Life and I am grateful that You've*
*sent Your son to die for me.*
*Father, I am content knowing that Your way is perfect. I am*
*content because You are by my side through it all.*
*In Jesus' Name, Amen!*

❊

## NOTES

------------------------------------------------

------------------------------------------------

------------------------------------------------

------------------------------------------------

------------------------------------------------

------------------------------------------------

------------------------------------------------

------------------------------------------------

------------------------------------------------

------------------------------------------------

------------------------------------------------

------------------------------------------------

------------------------------------------------

------------------------------------------------

------------------------------------------------

# PRAYER AGAINST DESPERATION

*Father, I pray that as I wait for the one You have for me that I will not become desperate. Help me not to be single and desperate. Even in this stage help me not to allow depression, sadness, or loneliness enter because that makes room for the enemy to come in to make me feel desperate and do desperate things.*

*Father, if I stay in Your word and stay praying every day I won't become desperate. Help me to hold fast to Your word and to wait on You. Help me to realize that if I enter a relationship out of desperation bad company ruins good morals (**1 Corinthians 15:33**). Help me to also realize that if I enter into a relationship out of desperation I could lose my identity, compromise, or lose You and I don't want any of that. I don't want to lose what we've built up together. I don't want to lose our relationship, so shake me and grab a hold of me when and if desperate times come.*

*Help me to take my time for when I become desperate I miss the signs. Help me not to throw myself into romance too soon or too fast. Help me not to be afraid of being single.*

*I command the spirit of desperation that is seeking to destroy*

*me to flee in the name of Jesus. Help me to be patient. Help
me to wait on You and not go seeking in my own strength.
Father, I make a promise right now that I will not date just
anyone. I will be lead by Your Spirit. I will hear Your
voice. I will be joyous. I will not be desperate for a man. I
will not force what doesn't fit. For I know You have the
relationship I desire and need and You will bring it. Help
me to be strong and wait for what I deserve. I will let Your
joy be my strength. I may be single but I am NOT
desperate.
In Jesus' Name, Amen!*

❄

NOTES

_____
_____
_____
_____
_____
_____
_____
_____
_____
_____
_____
_____
_____
_____
_____
_____

# PRAYER FOR PAST MISTAKES & SINS

*Father, I am sorry and please forgive me for my past mistakes and sins. I ask that You help me to forgive myself since You have already forgiven me. Forgive me for doing things against what You have commanded. Forgive me for going against Your will. I repent right now for any sexual sin, lust or anything against You that I have done.*

*Sin separates me from You. Adam and Eve tried to hide their sin and I don't want to hide it any longer. I come to You telling You about all of my sins and repenting of them. Father, as it says in **Psalm 51:10**, "Create in me a pure heart, O God, and renew a steadfast spirit within me." I now strive to live towards living a purposeful life in You instead of becoming like those in the world.*

*Lord, I pray that You would help me to now let go of my past completely. Deliver me from any hold it has on me. Help me to turn away from past habits and be renewed in my mind. Give me the mind of Christ so that I can hear Your voice rather than the voices of the past.*

*When the past tries to haunt me help me to remember that I am a new creation and old things have passed away (**2***

*Corinthians 5:17). If I continue to relive the past, I will hinder living in the new life You have given me. Help me get past the past. Help me to remember that the past is the past. My past holds no power over me since I am a new creature in Christ.*

*Lord, when You died on the cross You paid the price in full. I no longer will live in the past. I choose now to live in a new day, in Your day. I now shut the door on the past. I shut the door to sin. I shut the door to all wrongdoing to me and by me.*

*I won't go back to my past mistakes and sins. I receive Your forgiveness. Thank You, Lord, for forgiving me and helping me not to relive it or ever do it again.*

*In Jesus' Name, Amen!*

"*F*orget the former things; do not dwell on the past." **(Isaiah 43:18)**

❄

NOTES

_____
_____
_____
_____
_____
_____
_____
_____
_____
_____
_____
_____

# PRAYER FOR FORGIVENESS
# FOR EXES

*Father, help me to forgive my exes. Help me not to take on the view of the world such as I will forgive but I will not forget. For that is not forgiveness at all. Just like You forget and throw away my sins into the sea of forgetfulness when I repent, help me to do the same for my exes.*

*For You word says, for if You forgive other people when they sin against You, Your heavenly Father will also forgive you (**Matthew 6:14**). I need forgiveness so help me to forgive my exes that have wronged me. Help me to forgive the exes that have hurt me in previous relationships. Help me to not have any ill will towards my exes.*

*Help me to release the hurt and pain and begin to love as You love. Help me to see them through Your eyes. Father, allow Your Holy Spirit to fill my heart with Your peace. Help me find compassion that comes with true forgiveness.*

*I also ask that when and if I see my exes who have hurt me, remind me of this prayer so that I can take ungodly thoughts captive and make them obedient to Christ (**2 Corinthians 10:5**). Let them see a new me, a better me*

*that You've created. Let them see the joy of the Lord in me
because of this forgiveness and me letting go.*

*I thank You for the power of forgiveness and I choose right
now to forgive [name Your exes]. Help me set [name Your
exes] free and give all my burdens to You. Help me to bless
those who have hurt or harmed me. Help me to be kind
and compassionate to them, forgiving [name Your exes],
just as You've forgiven me.*

*I thank You and I give You glory for the work You are doing in
me. I thank You for helping me to be free from this. I thank
You for helping me to let go and to forgive.*

*In Jesus' Name, Amen!*

❄

*L*uke 17:3-4 So watch Yourselves. "If Your brother or sister sins against You, rebuke them; and if they repent, forgive them. Even if they sin against You seven times in a day and seven times come back to you saying 'I repent,' you must forgive them."

NOTES

----------------------------------------

----------------------------------------

----------------------------------------

----------------------------------------

----------------------------------------

----------------------------------------

----------------------------------------

----------------------------------------

----------------------------------------

----------------------------------------

----------------------------------------

# PRAYER FOR SINGLE MOTHERS

*Father, first I ask that you help me to stop believing the lie that no good man would ever want me with kids and all. I remove that lie over me and my family right now. I know that there is a good man willing to step up and love me and my child(ren). If you've done it for others, I know you'll do it for me too.*

*I believe right now that you already have a good Christian man for me. Nothing is too hard for You. For you have designed families to have a mother and a father and I thank you for sending the godly man who can accept and marry me and love my kid(s).*

*Pick the perfect mate for me and father to my child. Pick someone who I can grow together with. I pray for an anointed man of God that will be the head of the household. I pray for a man that loves you first because I know that if he loves You first, he'll love me and all I love.*

*I ask that you bless my family with everything we need. Sometimes it is hard being a single mother but I know that you will supply every need of mines according to Your riches in glory in Christ Jesus.*

*I pray that all the sadness I may have now will turn to
happiness soon. I trust that You will give me someone
someday. I pray for peace and happiness in every area of
my life. I won't be anxious about anything any longer for
You Lord are my rock, my fortress, my deliverer, and my
God, the one who will provide the desires of my heart.*
*In Jesus' Name, Amen!*

❄

NOTES

------------------------------------------------
------------------------------------------------
------------------------------------------------
------------------------------------------------
------------------------------------------------
------------------------------------------------
------------------------------------------------
------------------------------------------------
------------------------------------------------
------------------------------------------------
------------------------------------------------
------------------------------------------------
------------------------------------------------
------------------------------------------------
------------------------------------------------
------------------------------------------------
------------------------------------------------
------------------------------------------------

# INVITATION

If you have not accepted Jesus as your personal Lord and Savior, I invite you today to accept Him. Before it is too late, ask Him to come into your life and be your Lord and Savior. Recite this prayer:

> *Lord, I know that I am a sinner. I ask you today to come into*
> *my life to make me whole and to make me clean. I believe*
> *you died on the cross and rose three days later just to save*
> *me. I am eternally grateful. From this day forward, I*
> *promise to serve you and only you. I give my life, my*
> *heart, my soul, my mind, and my body to you. In Jesus'*
> *Name, Amen.*

If you have accepted Jesus as your personal Lord and Savior for the very first time or if you are rededicating your life to Christ, please go to sherylynnerochester.com or email me. I would like to stay in contact with you and I would like to send you some information about being saved. Congratulations and welcome to the kingdom of God.

# PLEASE WRITE A REVIEW

Without you, I don't have a readership ...

First, I want to thank you for reading this book all the way to the end. If you've enjoyed this book and can't wait to read the second installment, please write a five-star review. I want to get an initial set of reviews so I can take them into account. Then, get back in the trenches to add the "polish" and write some more.

Second, if you've enjoyed this book, please share it with someone else. Don't give the story away though, just tell them that they have to read this book. My goal is to encourage all those waiting on God to send them who He has for them. I believe this book will encourage singles especially single mothers or those raising kids in any function. So, you can share this book in so many ways. Just post on social media with the hashtag winter romance (#winterromance) of a quote you've enjoyed in the book or even take a picture of the book and tag a friend.

Again, I want to thank you for reading and purchasing A Winter of Romance. Just remember that God has a winter romance for you that you'll never forget. Have faith, don't doubt, and prepare for what's coming!

Your time is fast approaching ...

ALSO BY SHERYLYNNE L. ROCHESTER

Altered Destiny A Hustler's Choice

Altered Destiny Second Chance

Chronicles of a Vixen (Part 1)

God Send Me My Husband

Dear Husband Journal (Pink)

Dear Husband Journal (Purple)

A Winter of Romance

Save The Date

FREE STUDY GUIDE FOR GOD SEND ME MY HUSBAND
AT WWW.SHERYLYNNEROCHESTER.COM

COMING SOON

God Send Me My Husband on Audible

Save The Date on Audible

Save The Date Study Guide

# ABOUT THE AUTHOR

Sherylynne L. Rochester was born and raised in Brooklyn, New York. She has always had a love of music and while growing up in the city she spent a lot of time singing and writing songs while also being a member of the Girls' Choir of Harlem.

She attended Five Towns College in Dix Hills, Long Island, where she received her bachelor's degree in Business Management. It was at college that she discovered a passion for writing, something that has become a major part of her life. She has now penned numerous novels and a journal such as Altered Destiny: A Hustler's Choice, Altered Destiny: Second Chance, Chronicles of a Vixen, God Send Me My Husband, A Winter of Romance, and the Dear Future Husband Journal.

Now residing in beautiful Pennsylvania, where she is a minister and a Praise and Worship Leader at Prevailing Word Ministries (Brooklyn, NY), Sherylynne sees it as her duty to bring people closer to God through music and worship, helping them to find God and experience Him and the love He has for them.

When she isn't hard at work doing the will of God or working on her music and next novel, Sherylynne still loves to sing, is learning to play keyboard and guitar, writes almost daily and relaxes by watching TV, or reading.

Sherylynne was recently engaged in April 2016 to the love of her life. She waited for God to send her the right man after 14 years. That is why she has penned the novel, God Send Me My Husband and Save The Date, to help Christian Singles everywhere.

It is this deep faith, she is convinced, which has made her the success she is today. To date Sherylynne L. Rochester has sold over 60,000 books.

*Join Sherylynne's Mailing List:*
www.sherylynnerochester.com
author@sherylynnerochester.com

CPSIA information can be obtained
at www.ICGtesting.com
Printed in the USA
LVHW041927300920
667543LV00003B/576

9 781981 816385